Rosa's Truth

Joanie Smith

Rosa's Truth is a work of fiction. Any resemblance of any character to any other person, living or dead, is unintentional.

Wiltshire Books LLC

Huntington, West Virginia

Acknowledgments

If my great-grandmother and grandmother had been truthful human beings who married the fathers of their children, I wouldn't have a book to write. So, I must thank them and their strained relationship with the truth along with their willingness to perpetuate their less-than-honest stories.

I am blessed beyond my wildest imagination to be married to such a kind, loving and patient man, my husband, Gabe. He is proof that God exists. I appreciate his support, encouragement and his typo-spotting ability.

And then there's Ellen Brown Marcum. Grammar is her passion. I gave her hours of fun correcting mine. Thank you, Ellen, for your friendship and for understanding my semicolon aversion syndrome.

Do you know the difference between emigrate and immigrate? Cannoli versus cannolis? Michele Schiavone, my amazing editor, knows the difference. I am so grateful for her friendship, support, encouragement and help. Having said all that, I know she is receiving a kickback from the comma gods.

JB in the following story is my friend Janet Bailey. She is one of the most talented people I have been blessed to meet. Her enthusiasm and encouragement for all my creative endeavors mean the world to me.

Based on my family's true story, Rosa's Truth takes place in both the After Life and the Land of the Living. I have changed the names of the very guilty and the slightly naughty. I have changed the names of my cousins, the innocent and the understandably embarrassed.

Rosa's Truth offers plausible explanations for Great-grandmother Angelica's and Grandmother Rosa's lies, deceptions and misconceptions. When plausibility fails, I embellish. I embellish a lot. This fruit didn't fall far from the storytelling tree.

Dedicated with love and gratitude to

Mom and Aunt Aria

Rosa's Truth

Chapter One

"No, no, NO! this can't be happening," Rosa wailed. "What am I going to do? *What am I going to do?*" Rosa repeatedly asked herself while wringing her hands and pacing rapidly back and forth. "This cannot be happening."

Rosa Caserta had been in the After Life since 1959. This was 2021. No one ever questioned her about her life in the Land of the Living. That life was over. She had no desire to explain herself now. The After Life was very pleasant. There was time to think, reflect and examine your life in the Land of the Living. That was ok for some. Not so much for Rosa.

She would rather hang on to her version of her life. That did require effort, creativity and closed lips. Confide in no one. Trust no one with the truth. She was an expert at covering up her truth. Her lies were flawless. No one suspected anything. Everyone believed her story.

Until now. Time was not on her side. She already knew what was going on in the Land of the Living, others in her family might know, too. That was not acceptable. That would be unbearable. Her cover exposed, the truth revealed. "Never, not on my watch," muttered Rosa.

Not only was time not on her side, the rules in the After Life limited what she could do. The Two Big

Obstacles, as Rosa referred to them. Big Obstacle Number One: "You cannot interfere with the actions in the Land of the Living." Interference was forbidden regardless of how much you wanted to jump in to help. Or, in Rosa's case, regardless of how much she wanted to stop, thwart and prevent.

Big Obstacle Number Two: "You have to wait until you are asked for help before you can help." The After Lifers were allowed to communicate and nudge their loved ones in the Land of the Living. But they could not make people do or say something. They could not interfere with free will.

"Why can't I interfere—maybe just a little interference would be all I would need?" mused Rosa. "Surely there are loopholes. I need to find someone to help me."

Unfortunately, for someone to help, Rosa would have to tell the truth. She wanted to avoid that at all costs. Maybe she could confide in one of her many sisters. Rosa was one of ten children. She reviewed her siblings one by one. She disqualified every one of them. Some were too honest and would insist she tell the truth — the whole truth. Not happening. She hadn't been close to a couple of them in the Land of the Living, so they were out. She had an image to uphold. She could not let them see beyond her façade.

She couldn't turn to Antonio or Sal, her two husbands. That thought made Rosa almost laugh. As if Antonio would ever help her. *He* was the problem. Sal was too sweet and naive. She could never tell him.

"Oh dear, that just leaves *her*." Rosa was of course referring to her mother, Angelica Caserta. "This ought to be fun, actually, anything but fun. This could be disastrous."

Rosa and her formidable mother, Angelica, were not close now, and they hadn't been close in the Land of the Living. Rosa always suspected Angelica was hiding something. She was so guarded, so secretive and forlorn. Whatever her mother was hiding, she wasn't sharing it with Rosa. That sadness in Angelica's eyes, what was behind it? Rosa wondered whether the sadness might be connected to her distant, cold demeanor.

Her mother had forced her to leave Italy when Rosa was only 13 years old. Rosa wasn't ready to leave her family. She loved her dad and playing with her younger sisters and brothers. She didn't speak English. What was so wrong with her that her mother was getting rid of her? And now she needed that woman's help. She dreaded talking to her mother. Angelica who stood so straight, with such perfect posture, and her unbreakable veneer was unapproachable. Rosa was desperate. She needed someone who might know some loopholes in the rules of the After Life. Because Angelica had broken rules in the Land of the Living, she might know something Rosa could do. Rosa needed to interfere with her granddaughter, Emma, and her never-ending research into Rosa's family.

"Why can't that Emma just leave things alone? I told her cousins 'The Story.' It is a good story. Just leave it be," Rosa shouted. Anger and frustration filled her voice.

Rosa remembered telling "The Story" over and over to anyone who would listen. Always the same details in the same order. Just enough to answer the questions. Not too much to get caught in the details. Besides, how could anyone ever dispute her story? Anyone who might know bits and pieces of the truth was dead. If Emma would quit snooping around, Rosa's problems would go away. "The Story" would be safe and passed on to many more generations, just as Rosa had planned.

Rosa remembered the last time she saw her youngest granddaughter, Emma. Emma, at seven years old, was a little itty-bitty thing with big brown eyes. She stood in the hallway looking up at Rosa. Emma spoke English with a strange accent. A southern accent, some people called it. Rosa found it amusing. She wasn't finding Emma amusing now.

Emma was using some kind of machine—a computer machine or something. Whatever it was, it knew things about the family. Things Rosa didn't think anyone would ever find out. It was telling Emma these things.

Emma must be stopped regardless of the rules.

Chapter Two

I only have one memory of my Grandmother Rosa. I was seven or eight years old and she was standing in the hallway of her home in Pittsburgh looking down at me. She seemed tall and imposing with her arms folded across her chest. In reality, she was five feet two inches tall. I remember her white hair and a dark blue, short sleeved dress with a V-neck. She said something but it didn't sound like anything I'd heard before. I remember thinking, "She talks funny." I didn't realize my grandmother spoke English with an Italian accent. We lived in West Virginia, 250 miles from my grandmother, aunts, uncles and cousins. We saw them once a year, in the summer. I didn't know any of them very well.

Occasionally, Mom would tell me something about her family and her childhood. She was born in their small old house in a neighborhood comprised mostly of Italian immigrants. When she was seven years old, they moved up the hill to a larger and nicer house in a more diverse neighborhood. Her father was doing well with his railroad job. They also took in boarders for extra money.

I remember Mom saying, "Our next-door neighbors wouldn't let their kids play with us because we were Italian. They thought we were members of the Black Hand, the Mafia. We weren't, of course. I was too young to understand why they wouldn't play with us. I only knew we were being shunned." Mom seemed almost sad remembering the rejection.

I was pleased when Mom shared her memories with me. Our relationship was a rocky road filled with miles of ups and downs. Mom was frequently ill when I was a child. She was enmeshed in my sister's life when I was older. I was always the odd daughter out. My sister, Marianne, and I were the only children. Mom clearly preferred my older sister. I don't know why she did, I just always knew she did. Everybody knew her preference. I have stopped trying to figure out the reason for her noticeable preference. I've learned to live with it.

Rocky road or not, she was still my mother, and I wanted a closer relationship with her. I spent time thinking about how to accomplish this. Where could I find common ground? I thought if I understood her background, her childhood and early adult life, maybe I would understand her. If I understood her, maybe we could be closer. Maybe at long last she would finally approve of me—accept me—love me. Approval, acceptance and love are what I really wanted from my mother.

I was in my forties when I thought I would try one more time to get to know her. My life had changed dramatically. My dad, my buffer between me and Mom, had passed away. I ended a terrible, should-never-have-happened marriage. I returned to my hometown where my mother and sister still lived, and I remarried. This time to a man who is a saint and an angel wrapped up into one. He is indeed answered prayer. I felt safe in my marriage and in who I was. The time was right to put my "Get to Know Mom Plan" into action. I could have called it my "Please Love Me Plan."

I began my quest by asking Mom about her mother. I knew she adored her mother, Rosa Caserta Amorati Caserta. I thought this would be the logical place to start. I bought a piece of her favorite pie, coconut cream, to surprise her. Accompanied by my very cute little Lhasa Apso, Muffy, I knocked on her door. She was happy to see Muffy.

Mom was in a pretty good mood and didn't seem to mind the questioning. I guess the pie and Muffy were working. She explained her mother's past. "You remember Mom came to the United States when she was only 14 years old. She didn't speak any English. When she first arrived, she went to Youngstown, Ohio to live with her Aunt Louisa. They had already agreed that Aunt Louisa would find a husband for Mom. She knew all the Italian families in their community. She was frequently called upon to act as a matchmaker. Aunt Louisa arranged marriages, not love matches. She found my dad for my mom. They were introduced, the marriage was successfully arranged, and they were married." Mom told the story so casually as if this type of arrangement was an everyday occurrence. I guess it was, for Mom's mother, aunts and uncles. The ten of them kept Aunt Louisa busy.

I was shocked by her apparent acceptance of this. I couldn't conceive of such an idea. My grandparents had no input regarding whom they would marry. They were not given a choice. This wasn't like a television show where there are twenty contenders, and you get to pick one. A man was chosen for my grandmother. Mom said Grandmother Rosa was 16 years old when she married Antonio. They had nine children, six of whom lived to adulthood. I guess the marriage worked for them.

"What was your dad like?" I asked.

"My dad, Antonio, was a supervisor for the railroad. He was gone during the week. He came home on the weekends. He liked having lots of people around," my mother told me. "He played the accordion. There was always singing and dancing. He was fun. He liked to have a good time. He was an impeccable dresser. His clothes had to be a certain way and his shoes shined to perfection. His mustache was always trimmed and never a hair out of place. He expected the same from all of us.

"Dad liked to drink—he drank a lot. He died from stomach cancer in December, close to Christmas. I was ten years old. I'm the baby of the family. There were only three of us children left at home. Your Aunt Aria was 12 and Uncle Armani was 15." Mom just answered the questions. She rarely supplied lots of details. "My sister Minnie died right before Dad died. That was an incredibly sad time for all of us. Mom was alone with three children to raise and no income except the little money she made from the boarders."

"How did Grandmother Rosa meet Sal, your stepfather?" I was curious. Grandmother was in her 40's by then. Where would she go to meet a man? Would she even want to remarry? Had she been so in love with Antonio that no other man could live up to him?

"Well, your grandmother went back to Youngstown to Aunt Louisa. She wanted Aunt Louisa to find her another husband!" Mom almost laughed when she said this. I was pleased Mom was having fun. She didn't always like to answer questions about her family. "Aunt Louisa introduced Mom to another man, Salvatore Caserta. He was a distant cousin. That is why her maiden name and married name are the same. Her last names are Caserta Amorati Caserta. They were married in Ohio in Aunt Louisa's living room. Mom and Salvatore then returned to our home in Pittsburgh."

"Did you like him?"

"Yes, I liked him." Mom paused slightly, weighing her words. "He was quite different than my father. He was quiet. There were no more parties. The house was always very quiet." After a few more moments of reflecting how her life had changed when Rosa married Salvatore, Mom simply stated, "He was always nice to me and my brother and sisters. Mom seemed happy enough."

How strange, I thought. Two arranged marriages. The first arranged marriage was forced upon her. But the second marriage? She volunteered for that one. Not for me, thank you very much.

Mom appeared to be in a rare sharing mood. Good time to ask more questions. I was enjoying both the stories and Mom's talking to me. Maybe my plan was working.

"Did you know your grandmother?" I was trying to imagine my mother as a young child with her grandmother.

"I knew her. Her name was Angelica. She stood very straight. She had great posture." We have one picture of Angelica. She is indeed standing very straight as if at attention.

"When did she come to the States? Did she arrive with your grandfather?" I asked Mom.

"She immigrated to the United States after Mom had lived here for several years. She had 10 children in Italy. Then she moved to Pittsburgh. I think my grandfather had died and she decided to join her children here."

"Then what happened to her?" I wanted the conversation to continue. I kept asking questions.

"She met a man here and married him. They had two boys, my Uncle Alberto and Uncle Paolo. We called him Uncle Paul. I spent a lot of time with her when I was a young child. I took the train to her house when I was 12 to help take care of her. She was ill and died the next year. There was a big funeral with lots of people. She died a few years after my dad died."

"Grandmother had nine brothers and sisters?"

"Mom had six sisters and three brothers plus her two half-brothers."

For reasons I'll probably never know, Mom now seemed irritated with my questions. I thought it was odd she didn't want to talk about Angelica and her children. I realize now that Mom never mentioned the name of her grandfather. The conversation was over. Her lips were pursed. Walls were back up and the door closed on our relationship, again. I wondered why she was so guarded regarding her family's history. Was she hiding something?

After that one lovely afternoon spent with her, Mom no longer wanted to talk about her family. I knew she loved them. Maybe she was protecting this love by not sharing with me who these people were. She was almost evasive about their background. I was glad I had taken notes.

Shortly after my husband and I were married, my sister, Marianne, died unexpectedly. Mom died a few years later from a heart attack. I felt rootless. I didn't have an anchor. No parents, and my only sibling was gone. I was determined to research my ancestors. I needed roots, a sense of belonging.

Because all my aunts and uncles had also passed away, and we wanted to stay connected, my cousins and I started talking more often. I enjoyed this. The shared history and shared ancestors were important to us. We have developed a close relationship. Occasionally we talk about what we know about our grandparents and great-grandparents. All of us grew up with the same stories. We believed them. I wanted to fill in some of the blanks with facts. Facts like dates of arrival, naturalization dates, addresses, dates of births and deaths. I think this was my way of trying to be close to my mother and to keep the closeness I had enjoyed with my father.

So I joined an online ancestor research website. This allowed me with an opportunity to search immigration records, censuses, birth and death certificates and marriage licenses.

I had no idea what I was about to uncover.

Chapter Three

"Elaine called while you were out. She'd like you to call her as soon as possible. She has news!" announced my husband. He knew I'd be eager to return her call. Although he isn't into the whole ancestry thing as much as I am, he is supportive and encouraging.

Elaine and her brother, Andrew, and I are first cousins and close in age. They grew up a couple of blocks from our grandmother and step-grandfather. Elaine knew our grandmother much better than I did. I hoped she had remembered something about her. Eager for news, I quickly called Elaine.

Elaine had found her notes from a conversation with her dad, my Uncle Armani. He had died several years ago.

"Did you that know Grandmother Rosa didn't have a birth certificate? She needed one to register for Social Security."

That sounded impossible to me. Grandmother didn't have a birth certificate? How could she immigrate without one? How did she make it to 60 plus years old without this vital document? She didn't drive. I guess everything must have been in a husband's name.

I could hear the excitement in Elaine's voice. I knew this was going to be good. "Grandmother asked my dad to write a letter to her small town in Italy requesting her birth certificate." Grandmother Rosa didn't read or write Italian or English. My Uncle Armani spoke five different languages, and Italian was one of them.

"Dad told me when Grandmother opened the envelope with the birth certificate, she was horrified. 'Illegittimo' was stamped on her birth certificate. There was no father's name. Our grandmother is illegitimate. And wait! There's more! Dad gave me a list of Grandmother's sisters and brothers. They all have the same last name, Caserta. That is our great-grandmother's maiden name. All the children are illegitimate. All ten of them."

"Illegitimate" was resounding in my head. I was speechless. My mother's upbringing was so strict. My great-grandmother has a huge religious monument in the Catholic cemetery. Both my great-grandmother and my grandmother were very generous with their financial assistance to the Catholic Church. They attended Mass regularly—daily when they were older. Illegitimate! This didn't fit the persona they worked hard to establish and maintain.

"Oh!" was all I could manage. I was trying to pick my chin up off the floor. "Illegitimate?"

"I had forgotten that Dad had written this down. Grandmother was so upset about this and wouldn't talk about it. Dad never mentioned it again. I don't know if he ever told anyone. I don't know who saw the birth certificate. I can't imagine how embarrassed she must have been. She was always so proud. So morally uptight."

"Did she know she was illegitimate? Was this a surprise or an embarrassment?" I was so stunned I couldn't think.

Elaine thought for a moment before answering. "She had to know her parents weren't married. Her maiden name was her mother's maiden name. I think she was humiliated that now people would know. She was able to hide the truth before the birth certificate arrived."

"She had to show people that certificate to register to receive Social Security. I wonder what those people thought? This little sixty-five-year-old Italian lady dressed to perfection was illegitimate. Doesn't fit my picture of her. We need to talk to Diana. Does she know any of this?" Diana was our older first cousin. She was 17 years older than I. Growing up she spent every afternoon with Grandmother. Maybe Grandmother had told Diana stories we hadn't heard.

I called Diana. Not only did she know that all ten children were illegitimate, she knew more. Diana is the most delightful, kind and caring person you will ever meet. She is a marvel. And the stories she tells! She seems to always have the scoop on family stuff. Talking to her is a treat.

"Our Grandmother Rosa was the eldest of ten children," began Diana. "Her parents never married. Her father was a padron like a mayor—of their community. He was much older than our great-grandmother, Angelica. She was 16 and he was 32 when they met. He instantly fell in love with her. He left his wife and their eleven children to live with Angelica. His first family, the one with his wife, lived in poverty. Grandmother Rosa used to see them running in the streets. The children were never dressed very nicely. They wore old hand-me-down clothes and boots. Angelica's mother and father were angry and mortified because Angelica and this man never married. They disowned her. Her grandparents, though, loved her so much. They continued to be on her side and helped her financially.

"When Grandmother was 14, her parents put her on a ship to the United States. She was all alone. She went to Youngstown, Ohio. She had an aunt living there. The aunt's job was to arrange marriages. She arranged one for our grandmother."

This was the same story my mother had always told me—minus the ten illegitimate children, of course. The additional scoop was fascinating and shocking. I was enthralled. Diana continued her story.

"When each one of Angelica's children turned 14, she put them on a ship to the United States. Then they would go to Youngstown, to the same aunt. She found spouses for them. I think Angelica came with the two youngest children. She left the father of her children. She said he married someone else and had more children. I guess his first wife must have died. Angelica met Carlo in Pittsburgh. They were married and had two more children. I don't know them. Angelica had her grandparents' money. She was well off. She bought several cemetery plots and that large statue in the cemetery. When she died, she left all her money to her two sons who were born in Pittsburgh. She left our grandmother $5.00. That is what Grandmother charged per week for one boarder. I've never understood that."

"Diana, how do you know all of this?"

"My mother told me about the illegitimacy and his wife's children living in poverty. Our grandmother told me bits and pieces. I saw her every day. We could see the front of her house from our back porch. I would go to her house to visit every day after school. We had dinner there every Sunday afternoon. I loved our grandmother. The three of us, my mom, our grandmother and I were very close. They shared these stories with me. I never tired of hearing them."

I will confess, I thought it was odd that Grandmother Rosa shared her unconventional background with her daughter Antonia and granddaughter Diana. She had been so strict with my mother. My mother and her sister Aria were not allowed to date until after they graduated high school. Mom graduated high school in 1933. She had never been on a date or gone to a school function with a boy. I would save these thoughts for another time. I had so much swirling around in my head. I wondered if Diana knew more details.

"Do you know our great-grandfather's name?"

"Neither Mom nor Grandmother Rosa ever mentioned his name. They seemed impressed he was the mayor and from a prestigious family. Uncle Armani said it was Andrea. Andrea is Uncle Armani's middle name. He is named after his grandfather."

I had so many questions. Did my mom know all of this? Who was my great-grandfather? This means we have lots of half-relatives out there somewhere. Who are these people? What happened to his other children? His wife? Why did Angelica leave him? Did she finally realize he wasn't going to marry her? He left his wife for her. So many questions. Would I ever find the answers?

"I'll search online to see if I can find his surname. Maybe I can find out what happened to him. If I can find him, hopefully I'll find our great-great-grandparents, too." I was on the hunt for more pieces to our family history puzzle. I was hopeful I'd find answers, not more questions.

Chapter Four

Since Grandmother Rosa had nine brothers and sisters, I was sure someone related to one of her siblings would be researching the family. I was right. My search using my ancestry website revealed there were several other people researching our family name, Caserta.

The website I use allows members to see other members' public trees. I could look at these trees to see how these other researchers were related to me. Our relationship was through my grandmother's sisters and brothers. I searched through their trees hoping to find more information. There was information about Grandmother Rosa's siblings, who they married and their children.

Several of them had my great-grandfather's first name listed as Andrea. A couple of other researchers had his name listed as Andrea Caserta. They listed Angelica's maiden name as his surname. Finally, my time and efforts paid off. There, on my computer screen was a last name and a fuzzy, overexposed picture of Andrea Diserta with one of his sons. I was thrilled. Great-grandfather, my mystery man. We meet at long last.

Thankfully, I could contact my fellow researchers, my new cousins, via the website. The excitement of the treasure hunt for puzzle pieces and the thrill of discovery was real. I was looking and hoping for more information. I hoped someone would know all about my newly discovered great-grandfather. I wondered if they knew the same story about the ten illegitimate children and the married older man who was their father. What stories did they know?

A few of them responded. They were great-grandchildren of my grandmother's siblings. We started corresponding and sharing information. However, none of them had heard "The Story," as I referred to it. I did feel a little weird sharing such an unflattering picture of our ancestors. They knew all Angelica's children had her maiden name as their last name. Only one of my new cousins had a last name for Angelica's live-in love. She was the one who had the picture of her great-grandfather with Andrea. Unfortunately, there was no one still living in her family who could confirm the parentage or provide additional information about Andrea. I had no new information about him.

Based on this information, as sketchy as it was, we decided Andrea Diserta was the man who fell madly in love with Angelica. He was so in love he left his wife and 11 children to live with Angelica and have 10 more children with her. I would really like to talk to him. What was his side of the story? Was he a father figure to his "other" children? How did he justify his liaison with Angelica?

I frequently wonder if we will have all our questions about our lives answered when we pass over to the After Life. I fervently hope so. I wonder if I will meet my great-grandfather in the After Life. I have been told and have read in many books that when we die, we are met by the people we have loved while living. I hope this includes great-grandparents I have never met but owe my existence to. If my great-grandparents had not put my Grandmother Rosa on that ship in 1896, I wouldn't be here today.

Chapter Five

I was so excited to call Elaine to tell her the good news. "We have a great-grandfather! I have found him. His name is Andrea Diserta. And I have a photo of him. It is fuzzy, but there he is. The man with 11 children by his wife and 10 by our great-grandmother Angelica. "

My excitement was obvious. I was bubbling over with thoughts I needed to share.

"I think it's kinda crazy. He had all those children with his wife by the time he was 32. Or do we think he continued to see his wife after he met Angelica? Was he sleeping with his wife and our great-grandmother? Whatever was Angelica thinking? He was wealthy and he was a somebody. I wonder if she fell instantly in love with him, too?"

I was talking so fast, Elaine couldn't get in a word.

"He couldn't divorce his wife because there were no divorces for Catholics then. No divorce because she was Catholic—but she would 'live in sin' with a married man?"

Whew! I had to pause to catch my breath.

Elaine managed to take advantage of my much-needed pause. "You know Angelica's parents were so furious and disappointed in her they disowned her. I wonder did they know their grandchildren? Did they talk to them? Play with them? Or were they disowned, too? Maybe Diana knows if Grandmother Rosa knew her grandparents. Do you think Angelica sent her children to the United States because of her scandalous behavior? She didn't want people talking about them or ostracizing them."

Elaine is a grandmother of five. She loves being "Grammie." I wasn't surprised that she would think about the grandchildren's/grandparents' relationship. Those were valid questions. I would love to talk to my grandmother and great-grandmother right now.

I added more questions. "Why did Angelica decide to leave Andrea and emigrate? They had ten children together. What happened to Andrea? Did he die and she wanted a new life in a new country? A geographical cure?"

Elaine added a few more details. "According to the story Grandmother told Diana, he married someone and had more children. I guess his first wife must have died. So, he was free to remarry. My dad didn't know that part of the story. We always guessed Andrea had died and then Angelica emigrated."

We continued to talk about the limited facts that we knew. We had oral family history but nothing to prove it. We finally had a last name for Andrea. But what was next? Was there anything else we could research or do to find more answers? A search for more information on my online ancestry website provided nothing more about him. Outside of the Caserta family tree, Andrea Diserta didn't exist.

We seemed to be at a standstill. I was looking at my computer while talking to Elaine so I could keep the facts straight. I saw our next step on my screen.

"Let's do a DNA test. Maybe we will find more relatives. Relatives with answers."

While we waited for our DNA results, I continued to research our family. I found a few censuses for my grandparents. I was so excited. There they were in Pittsburgh, 1910, with four of their children. My Aunt Aria and my mom hadn't been born yet. I'm not sure of the reason, but I was so touched by seeing the names of my aunts and uncles on the census. They became real to me. My Uncle Armani was an infant. So curious to think of someone as accomplished as my uncle as an infant. I thought all of this was endearing. The census contains so much information. I already knew some of it. Birthplace was Italy, language spoken was Italian. I knew my grandmother could neither read nor write English or Italian. Everything was as expected until I read, "Age at first marriage." My grandmother had responded "14." She was only 14 years old when she was married off to a 19-year-old man-child she barely knew. This was news. Perhaps that is why I couldn't find a marriage license. Maybe there wasn't one.

I thought about myself at age 14. I certainly was not emotionally mature enough to even be away from my parents. Marriage at that age was out of the question. I can't begin to imagine what Grandmother Rosa experienced. Thousands of miles from her small town of 1,200 in Italy where she lived surrounded by her brothers and sisters, her parents and dozens of cousins, Rosa was basically on her own in a very large foreign city. I worried about how she adjusted to all the changes in her life. I worried about her going to bed with her husband, Antonio. Was she frightened? Did she have a clue about what was going on? My heart ached for this young and inexperienced girl. I hoped my grandfather, Antonio, was more experienced in life and in bed and was good to her.

I searched and searched for their marriage license. The county in Ohio where I thought they had married had a genealogy research volunteer on staff. I contacted her. She searched their records using various spellings and lots of possible dates but found only my grandmother's sister's marriage license. There was one curious note about her license. Their father's name was listed as Andrea Caserta and not Andrea Diserta. Caserta was definitely Angelica's maiden name. Did she think her parents were married? Was she hiding the fact that they weren't married? Didn't she know he had a different last name? Again, so many questions.

I wanted to talk to Diana. I wanted to double check the family oral history. Perhaps I had misunderstood how old Grandmother Rosa was when she married. We were told she was 16.

In addition to the censuses, my research included finding the passenger lists which provided information about who immigrated and when. Now I really needed to talk to Diana. Again, there was conflicting information.

"You found the date when Rosa immigrated?" asked Diana. "She was 14 when she arrived in the United States."

"I did find the passenger list. Grandmother Rosa immigrated when she was 13, not 14. There are two other people on the passenger list from the same small town going to Youngstown, Ohio. There is a woman and a young boy. The young boy has the same last name as our grandmother. I'm trying to find out more about them."

"Grandmother always told me when each child turned 14, they were put on a ship to the United States. Great-grandmother Angelica came last with the two youngest." Diana repeated the same story she had told me when I first started my research. This is the story we grew up with and accepted as our family's history.

I wasn't sure how to tell Diana that none of that was true. Her mother had told her these stories and our grandmother had reinforced them. The account of the immigration of the Caserta family simply wasn't true. Giving my grandmother the benefit of all doubts, I rationalized that she had forgotten when her siblings arrived. She was married and a young mother with lots of responsibilities. Remembering immigration dates wasn't one of these responsibilities. Yet, this bothered me. Surely their arrival was a time of celebration. This would have been her chance for Rosa to show off her house, her husband Antonio, and her daughter, Antonia. She could help them with their English and their assimilation into American culture.

"I found the passenger lists for Rosa's siblings," I explained to Diana. "The truth is they arrived in groups. This first group included three sisters. They arrived in 1899. The second group is somewhat of a surprise. Our great-grandmother Angelica immigrated with the three youngest children. She went straight to Pittsburgh after she arrived. This was in 1901. The youngest was just an infant. The remaining three children immigrated two years after their mother, in 1903. I guess they lived with their father until they immigrated."

Diana was quiet for a moment. The conflicting information was bewildering.

"That isn't what Grandmother told me. Why would she tell me something that wasn't true? Why didn't she tell me the truth? Why did Grandmother tell me those stories? She and Mom both told me the same story about the immigration dates, ages and marriages. This doesn't make sense. Maybe she just forgot the details? How could Angelica leave three of her children in Italy?"

Neither Diana nor I had any answers to these questions. Was Rosa attempting to hide the truth or did she have a faulty memory?

Chapter Six

"How is your research going?" asked my husband. I'm not sure how interested he really was, but he does enjoy a good story. And this story was getting good.

"Seems Grandmother Rosa either had a poor memory or she was a revisionist. She didn't immigrate when she was 14. She was 13. She didn't marry when she was 16. She was only 14. She is not from 'Caserta.' She is from a small town 20 miles from Caserta. She also told Diana that her siblings immigrated when they turned 14. According to her, each sibling traveled alone. The passenger manifests tell a different story. They traveled in groups. Perhaps the most confusing part is that Great-grandmother Angelica left three children in Italy and immigrated before they did. How could she leave three small children behind? She arrived a couple of years before they did. She traveled with the three youngest. One was just an infant. So much for her story. I wonder what else isn't true?"

I've always admired my husband for his ability to listen to and usually understand both sides of a story. I was curious what he was thinking.

"Maybe your grandmother just had incomplete recollections. Which is understandable. There are lots of details to remember regarding her family's immigration records. If this isn't the case, she must have had a good reason to fabricate a story. Perhaps she is trying to protect someone."

"Protect whom and why? The true story based on the facts is fine. A little confusing about how she could leave three children in Italy. Maybe they just wanted to live there. The untruths do nag at me. There are so many misrepresented details." I was having a difficult time calling them lies. I struggled with what to call them.

"There is a plausible explanation," he said. "Married at 14 is not acceptable now. I guess things were different in 1887. Maybe she lied about her age to the priest who married them. Maybe she was so in love with your grandfather, she couldn't wait!"

I appreciated his attempt to explain my grandmother's actions.

"Is this the grandmother who had seven illegitimate children?" he asked.

"That was my great-grandmother. Ten children born without the benefit of their parents' marriage. But who's counting after seven? My grandmother was married to the father of her children." I added proudly, "The fruit fell far from that free-spirited tree!"

Chapter Seven

Rosa dreaded meeting with her mother, but Rosa was desperate. Her lies were going to catch up with her. She hoped her mother would help her interfere with Emma's research in the Land of the Living. Maybe just some harmless interference like snipping some wires in the computer machine. Does a computer machine have wires? Rosa didn't know. Anyway, she needed to do something to stop Emma.

Her mother, Angelica, was waiting for her. Standing at attention and looking stern, Angelica barely had time to greet her daughter before Rosa exclaimed, "Mother! Something dreadful has happened!"

Rosa was hesitant to tell her mother this awful news. They weren't close and they didn't confide in one another. Even now in the After Life, their conversations were mostly shallow and insignificant. Occasionally, when they were in the Land of the Living, they shared a recipe or two. That was about all the sharing there was between mother and daughter before and after death.

"I don't know what to do. This is awful! My nosey little granddaughter, Emma, is snooping around and asking a lot of questions."

"Remind me again, which one is Emma?"

"Emma is the daughter of my youngest child. Emma is Marianne's sister. You know Marianne. She is here in the After Life with us."

"Oh, yes, that Marianne! She is a hoot!"

"Mother, whatever does that mean?"

"People in the Land of the Living say that when something or someone is funny. Marianne told me that. I love talking to her."

"Please! Focus. I need your help." Rosa had never asked her mother for help with anything.

Angelica was intrigued by this cry for help. Something serious must be going on for Rosa to reach out to her. Angelica was touched by this. She listened with uncharacteristic gentleness.

"I know we have passed over to the After Life and we have guidelines and limitations regarding how we can help our loved ones who are still in the Land of the Living. We want to help but we can't eavesdrop or spy on their lives. We have to wait for them to ask us for guidance. However, I think this situation calls for interference and serious eavesdropping." Rosa was desperate.

"What are you talking about, Rosa? We love to hear from the Living. We are allowed to nudge them, to whisper to them. We can't interfere but we can be around them. During some special times the Living can feel our presence. That ability is a gift we have been given. Eavesdropping? Unacceptable."

"I know, but this is different. We need to interfere this time. Emma has a device that she uses. It is called a computer machine, I think. Somehow, she touches letters on a board while looking at something like a small television. And then suddenly she knows things. The computer machine knows stuff about our family. Emma found out when I immigrated. She knows when you immigrated. You remember our names were written down when we boarded the ship?"

"Yes, a passenger list. They asked several questions about where we were from and where we were going," answered Angelica.

"Did you know they kept those lists? Why would they keep them? Who would care about such dates? The computer machine has all those lists. Emma found out when all of us immigrated." Rosa couldn't imagine why anyone would care about those passenger lists.

"She is inquisitive. She seems to like that sort of thing, although I don't know why. I still don't understand why you think this is a problem."

Rosa was slow to respond. She was in trouble. What she thought had been harmless fun was coming back to haunt her. Rosa was never proud of her childhood or her parents. She was embarrassed by the life her mother had chosen. When Rosa's children had asked questions about her life in Italy, Rosa had embellished a few things, tossed in an untruth or ten, and left out some things. Emma was uncovering the truth beneath Rosa's tall tales, and Rosa was terrified. She must take some action. But what kind of action? She never confided in her mother. She didn't even really like her mother. She certainly didn't understand her—nor did she want to understand her. Rosa just wanted some help. Surely her own mother would help her. After all, this involved her, too. She was actually the cause of Rosa's problem with Emma's discoveries.

Chapter Eight

"You know my family knows I am illegitimate. The terrible birth certificate revealed it. 'Illegittimo' was stamped on it. Really, Mother. Lots of questions were asked. I told my eldest daughter and my only son the truth—all ten of your children were illegitimate. Then I began to improvise. I told them I immigrated when I was 14, not 13. I also told them that you waited until each of my siblings was 14 and sent them to America one by one. I added that you came over with the two youngest. Emma has found out that my story isn't true."

"Why didn't you just tell them the truth? What was so bad about the truth that you had to make up a story?" asked Angelica.

"So many reasons. I was ashamed of you. You left three of your children in Italy. What kind of mother does that? You abandoned them." Rosa was clearly angry with Angelica. She hadn't realized how angry she was with her mother until she spoke those words. Resentment raged in her heart. Rosa remembered being sent to America on her own. Forced abandonment. She was furious. "I told them you sold Beni to a farmer because the farmer needed help on the farm."

Angelica remained calm, surprisingly calm. She listened and only added one comment, "Beni was an infant."

"I made it up because I was angry at you. I wanted to make you look bad. I didn't think anyone would believe me, but they did. That's not all." Rosa took a deep breath.

Rosa had never admitted to herself how angry she was at her mother. She was surprised at the anger's power over her. She had viewed her relationship with her mother through this lens of anger and resentment. This prevented them from having a healthy relationship. Harboring the anger and resentment drained Rosa of her ability to see the good in her mother and in herself.

Looking straight into her anger, Rosa told it she no longer wanted it in her heart and soul. The anger served no purpose in her life either here or in the Land of the Living. She let go of her need to hang onto the anger. She had faced her anger and she did not disappear into it. She was stronger than the anger. Her desire for healing was stronger than the power she had given her anger.

She felt her anger start to dissolve. This would take time, but Rosa was healing. She felt a calmness fill her being. And it felt good.

Something else happened, too. Rosa realized she wanted to tell her mother the whole truth. She didn't want to hide behind the untruths and embellishments any longer. Rosa had perpetuated the story with so many people for so many years. She spread this tale to her siblings' children and grandchildren, too. She was tired of living with her self-inflicted dishonesty and the constricting web of deception. She had never felt this way before.

"There is more to this story. I said that our community was named after our family, Caserta."

"Rosa! There is a small town named Caserta, but it has nothing to do with us."

"I know, but it made us sound important. I wanted them to think we were important and prestigious," Rosa responded sheepishly.

"Is there more to this tall tale?"

The truth of her storytelling and lies tumbled out of Rosa. The dam of years of deception had been unleashed. The truth was finally set free.

"I also made up a story about my father. I said he was the mayor of our community. He was from a very wealthy and influential family. They owned a magnificent palazzo on top of the hill. When he was 32 you were only 16. He saw you walking down the street. He took one look at you and thought you were the most beautiful woman he had ever seen. He instantly fell madly in love with you. There was only one problem. He was already married and had 11 children with his wife. According to my story, he left his wife to live with you. He couldn't get a divorce because divorces were forbidden by the Catholic Church."

"He couldn't divorce but we could live together in sin?" Angelica was stunned by this tale her daughter was telling her. "He had 11 children by one woman and 10 more with me? How is that even possible? More importantly, why would you say such things?"

"I thought the story was tragically romantic. The two of you were so in love! You didn't care what others thought. Living in sin didn't matter as long as the two of you were together." Rosa liked her version of the story.

"Go on," murmured Angelica. Rosa had unwittingly hit a nerve with her mother.

"I added some other details, too. I said that my father's wife and his first family were disgraced and forced to live in poverty. They wore tattered hand-me-downs and old boots. They couldn't afford shoes. I saw the children playing in the street because they had no other place to play."

Angelica cringed. Rosa was painting Angelica as a heartless husband-stealing woman who caused pain and misery in the lives of 11 children. "What kind of a monster does she think I am?" she wondered to herself. She needed to proceed cautiously. Her daughter was not accustomed to sharing her emotions or concerns with her. Angelica wanted Rosa to continue. This was all new territory for both of them. She wasn't sure why Rosa was telling her all of this, but she was glad. Maybe this could be the beginning of a more authentic relationship with her daughter.

She hoped the walls between them were coming down.

"Does this desperately-in-love-with-me-mayor have a name?" Angelica was almost afraid of what the answer might be.

"All I said was his name was Andrea."

"Why Andrea?"

"I like the name. No other reason. They asked for a name and I gave them one."

"Why didn't you tell them about your real father? You loved him." Angelica was trying with more patience than usual to understand Rosa's motivation for her lies and deception. "Explain to me why you invented a story."

"There is nothing romantic or special about being the daughter of a part-time fisherman who worked so hard on our farm. My father was wonderful and I loved him, but I wanted an intriguing story about my illegitimate birth. I have lived with that stigma of illegitimacy my whole life. I was embarrassed that you weren't married. I needed a reason why you two were never married. Can't you understand that? I thought a tragic love story of an older, prestigious married man was a good answer. I didn't care if the story made you look bad. Making you look bad was a bonus."

Rosa was filled with remorse and sorrow. "I regret telling those stories. I am so sorry I hurt you."

Angelica was tender and thoughtful in her response. "I've learned many things in the After Life. I know how important forgiveness is. When you forgive someone, you regain your power to give love. Forgiveness is for-giving. For-giving to yourself another opportunity to see that person in a new and different light. For-giving to yourself another opportunity to see *yourself* in a new and different light. I forgive you, Rosa. I hope you forgive yourself."

Rosa heard and embraced her mother's kind insights. She wanted to be free of the anger, the resentment, the lies. She wanted to be free of "The Story."

Forgiveness can take time, even in the After Life. The stories did pierce Angelica to her very essence. Her soul was wounded, and her heart ached. "Whatever have I done to her?" Angelica whispered to herself with a painful sigh, "I'm afraid the truth would hurt Rosa even more than her lies have hurt me. I don't know if I can ever tell her the truth about her father and me."

Chapter Nine

Angelica spent time contemplating Rosa's tall tale, "The Story," as they referred to it. She accepted her role in their relationship. She knew she had been distant and unavailable to her daughter. She needed to explain why.

She planned on talking to Rosa today. She wanted this new sense of closeness to grow. She wanted a healthy mother-daughter relationship with Rosa. She was pleased they had started their healing journey.

"I'm sorry my actions caused you pain and embarrassment." Angelica's apology to Rosa was sincere. "I'm beginning to understand that my actions impacted other people's lives as much as they impacted mine. I'm sorry I was so self-absorbed and unapproachable." She had spoken from her heart—a heart filled with unexpressed love for her daughter.

Rosa was clearly affected by her mother's apology. There were tears in her mother's eyes and her voice was filled with emotion. The years of Rosa's pent-up anger and resentment continued to melt. Rosa felt lighter. A weight had been lifted from her soul. Her heart opened a little to allow Angelica a small entrance. Allowing her mother in would take time. Nevertheless, the healing between mother and daughter had begun.

"Mom." Rosa never called Angelica "Mom." She had always used the more formal "Mother" to emphasize her distant relationship with her mother. Now, she wanted to call her "Mom" as a sign of closeness. "I forgive you. I'm sorry for making up the stories. I so deeply regret that they made you look bad—and regret even more that I hurt you. I'm so sorry." Rosa had tears streaming down her face. She completely understood what pain her lies inflicted. She also understood the confusion they were causing her family who was still in the Land of the Living.

For the first time since Rosa was a very young girl, Angelica and Rosa hugged. Maybe the After Life helped with this moment. Their relationship would never be the same. They were on their way to a mutually nurturing relationship filled with love and kindness. They weren't there yet. There was more to be resolved. There were lots more "stories" to come. With each story came the need to forgive. With each act of forgiveness came healing and spiritual growth.

"Would now be a good time to tell you the rest of the story? And explain why I am so worried about what Emma is going to discover?" Rosa wanted and needed her mother's help. The desire to be open and honest with Angelica filled Rosa's heart.

"There's more? Let me make sure I understand what has happened. Emma, your granddaughter, is researching our family history. She knows you and your siblings are illegitimate. You created an elaborate tale about your father. You said he was Andrea, the very married, wealthy mayor, aged 32 when I was 16. He had 11 children with his wife and 10 with me! Very busy man! Oh, and he left his wife to live with me. He couldn't divorce her. They lived in poverty, and we didn't. Do I have that right?"

"Yes, but more has happened. And this is where I need your help. There are two more problems. Emma has been using the computer machine again. I don't understand how that thing works, but somehow, she has been in touch with some of my siblings' grandchildren and great-grandchildren. Emma has shared the story about you and the supposed Andrea." Rosa paused, waiting for Angelica's reaction.

"Oh, dear," sighed Angelica, "there is no one in the Land of the Living to correct this story. All of our family members are living with this lie." Angelica thought this story might be better than the actual truth. The truth that none of her children knew, not even Rosa. You live and die with your secrets. Your lies require your friends and family in the Land of the Living to clean up your mess or to live in confusion and pain.

"Rosa, do you have any ideas how we can help? You know we cannot interfere. People in the Land of the Living have to ask for our help. Even then we are limited as to what we can do."

"There is one more part to this problem that I haven't told you. One of your children had his picture taken with Andrea Diserta. Do you remember that?" asked Rosa.

"Andrea was a neighbor. I remember there was a traveling peddler who had a camera. Bruno begged to

49

have his picture taken. Andrea was so good natured. He agreed to pay for the photo of the two of them. He had his photo taken with his parents, too. What does this have to do with anything? That was generous of Andrea. How could that be a problem?"

"Andrea, Mom, Andrea. They think this is THE Andrea. They think he is the mayor who fell in love with you! They think he is my father—the father of all 10 of us!"

Angelica was laughing. Rosa couldn't believe it. "This is serious."

"Why should this be a problem? This photo makes your story sound real. I don't like your story, but this could put an end to Emma's research. She has a name and a photo as confirmation—a nice added bonus. This should finish it. Although you do need to make amends with Andrea and his family."

"I'll make amends. I'll do my best to find them here in the After Life." Rosa was sincere in her intentions.

"Problem solved?" Angelica was sure they had put this behind them.

"No. I wish it were that simple. One of the great-grandchildren found Andrea Diserta's death certificate. They know he died 'unmarried.' My story is falling apart with this information. How could he have been married to his wife, have 11 children with her, yet die 'unmarried'? To make this even worse, his parents' names are on the death certificate. So they think they are their great-great-grands."

"Maybe they will think it is a mistake. Maybe his wife died before he did. Therefore, technically, when he died, he was unmarried. A clerical error. How could they prove otherwise? I don't think this is a problem. Who can they ask? No one," Angelica said.

Rosa was relieved. She hoped her mother was right. Too bad they couldn't predict the future. The future cannot be changed by anyone in the After Life, but they could have at least been prepared for what was coming next.

Chapter Ten

"This is interesting!" I interrupted my husband's fantasy football statistics scrutiny for the umpteenth time. "I have an email from someone in Italy who wants information regarding my mom's stepfather, Sal. He says he is related to him."

"Uh huh," responded my husband with less than great attention.

"This is good news. Sal was a distant cousin to my grandmother. They were married when Mom was around 10 years old. I haven't found out much about him online." I always welcome another piece of the puzzle when I am researching ancestors. I'd like to think my husband is as excited as I am.

"Oh, good, Honey." I think he was just glad I was finally going to leave him in peace while I rushed off to answer the email.

"Dear Francesco,

I don't know very much about Salvatore Caserta. I'll share what I do know. Here is a compilation of stories my mother and cousins have told me:

My grandfather died in 1925. My grandmother, Rosa Caserta Amorati, still had three children living at home. Her dream was to provide a college education for her one son, Armani. She needed financial assistance. In her mind, she needed a husband to help pay for Armani's education. Her sister lived in another state, Ohio, and was a matchmaker. Rosa went to Ohio to ask her sister to find a husband for her. Your grand-uncle, Salvatore, was living in Ohio. The aunt arranged a meeting, and the two decided to marry. I don't think this was a love match. They returned to Pittsburgh where Sal found a job in a steel mill. Mom has never said an unkind word about Sal. He provided for the three children and Rosa. What do you know about him?"

I was eager for a response. I had met Sal, but I was too young to remember much about him. I do remember he was sick, in a bed in the living room. I wasn't allowed in the room. My dad would sit by Sal's bed and talk to him. I would love to have heard those conversations. My dad was born in a holler in West Virginia, population 15. I wasn't sure where Sal had lived in Italy. He spoke with a thick Italian accent. I was told he had been a prisoner of war in Africa. I doubt the two had much in common, but my dad could talk to anyone.

Francesco responded with a request for pictures of Sal. I had only a few. There is one sweet one of Sal holding my hand, we were climbing the stairs into his house. I was five. I don't remember anything about the picture. I emailed the few pictures I had and asked if he knew that Sal had been a prisoner of war. I remembered Mom said Sal had wanted to be a priest. But he had killed people in the war. This scarred him for life. He didn't think he was worthy of being a priest. I always thought that was sad.

Francesco said he didn't know anything about this. Evidently, Francesco's grandfather, Sal's brother, had lost touch with Sal. The family knew very little about his life. I was happy to supply the few details I knew.

I realized I knew very little about Sal. Mom said he was quiet. There were no more parties in the house. No more accordion playing. Her father, Antonio, played the accordion and loved to fill the house with people. He also loved to drink. Sal didn't drink to excess, though he did make wine in the basement.

I don't know who held him captive during the war—or how he escaped or was released. Francesco said he had never heard of the story.

Then came the strange and somewhat shocking news. Francesco had Sal's family tree, of course. Sal was not my grandmother's distant cousin. He was her first cousin, once removed (his father was Angelica's first cousin). He explained that first cousins did marry in Italy during that time period. I wasn't so concerned about the first-cousin-once-removed-part as I was about yet another untruth. One more part of the story that was fabricated. Another cover-up? Why?

I'm not sure I'll ever know why Sal and Rosa were married. Why would he take on the responsibility of three children, a wife, boarders and a house? Why would he step into Antonio's shoes?

"Maybe after I pass over to the other side, I'll find answers," I mused to myself. "I hope so."

Francesco and I continued to email. He offered to send more information about Angelica's family. So my family tree grew. I was from a long line of Casertas who had lived in that small town since 1600. I found it so charming that I had a cousin who lived in my grandmother's hometown. He very kindly emailed pictures of the area where the family lived. I was feeling a real connection to Rosa and Angelica. I am grateful for Francesco's thoughtfulness in sending pictures. I told him the story about Angelica and the padron and ten illegitimate children. Again, he told me that he didn't know that story. Those things were not discussed. He offered to research information about my great-grandfather, Andrea Diserta.

Chapter Eleven

There are no clocks or calendars in the After Life. Time does not exist in the same form as it does in the Land of the Living. Angelica was grateful for this. She needed to think and reflect about Rosa's elaborate fabrication about her daughter's supposed father.

Some of it was almost humorous. The mayor? Stodgy old Mr. Agnello? That would take some imagination to put the two of us together. He was at least in his 60's when he was mayor. And Andrea Diserta. Nice man but a confirmed bachelor. He never dated, never married. He seemed to be happy hanging around his male buddies.

The humor ended there. Angelica was deeply concerned about Rosa's need to make up "The Story." She didn't want to label it a "lie," but what Rosa had told her daughter was a lie. Angelica knew all about lies. She was familiar with the heavy burden of living with them. She knew the barriers one must put up to protect them. She knew the destruction these barriers cause in relationships. She was weary of the barriers and destruction.

Lies still exist in the After Life if you choose to keep them. The choice is yours. If you want to continue on your path, your journey to wholeness, telling the truth is an essential step. You have all the time you need to arrive to your safety zone of truth telling. Angelica was finally there. Forgiving herself and the desire to tell her truth was all that was required to enter her safety zone in the After Life. She could continue her healing process.

She could have accomplished this in the Land of the Living, but the fear of judgment and rejection was too strong. Fear in the Land of the Living is frequently misunderstood. Angelica discovered that this fear isn't that other people might judge or reject you. This paralyzing fear is your judgment and rejection of yourself. Healing cannot take place in an environment of self-rejection.

Angelica was accepting her truth. She was facing her own judgment and rejection. She knew her journey would begin with Emilio.

Angelica remembered every detail about the first time she met Emilio. Those precious memories were etched into every fiber of her being. She had relived them during rare quiet moments and endless restless nights.

She was 22 years old and certainly old enough to be married. Her parents were urging her to settle down. They had someone in mind for her. His name was Giovanni, age twenty-four, a local boy from a good family with a good name. He worked on his family's farm.

Both families thought this was an advantageous match. Giovanni's family had money. He would inherit the farm, the large house, the barns and all the farm animals. That was an impressive inheritance.

Angelica would have standing in the community. She would be able to take care of her parents. A secure financial future for them would be assured with the marriage of their daughter to Giovanni.

His family would be gaining invaluable help with household chores and an expert seamstress. Angelica was experienced in milking cows and churning butter. The families hoped for many grandchildren.

Angelica liked Giovanni but she didn't feel a connection with him. Not the kind of connection that filled the longing in her body and soul. Your soul's longing was not anything parents took into consideration in 1880, in a small town in southern Italy.

Jobs were scarce. The toll of poverty on neighboring families was devastating. Men were emigrating to America to look for jobs. Many of them were sending much needed money home to their families in Italy. More and more men were staying in America and moving their families with them.

Her parents wanted Angelica to stay in Italy and marry Giovanni, the hard-working heir to the family fortune. She could forget this nonsense of her soul being touched.

Sunday Mass was a family event. Giovanni and his family would be there. Angelica's parents thought this would be the perfect time to lay the groundwork for the union of Angelica and Giovanni. Angelica knew what her parents were hoping for that day. She dreaded the whole thing. The very thought of the arrangement robbed her of her humanity—made her into nothing more than an entity with no thoughts and desires of her own. She didn't like being a commodity to be traded. "Here, you can have my daughter as long as you promise we won't have to provide for her any longer, and she'll be able to provide for us when we are old." That is what they were thinking, why not just be honest and say it? Angelica felt physically and spiritually ill at the thought of this dehumanizing custom.

Father Umberto, long time parish priest and friend of the family, greeted them with more than his usual cheerfulness. He approved of the possible match. He was in on the plan and was there to facilitate, hence the cheerfulness. Angelica knew he was up to something.

Standing next to Father Umberto was another priest, his back was turned to Angelica. "Great! Father Umberto has brought in reinforcements," sighed Angelica to herself. Her fate was sealed. She was doomed to an arranged, loveless marriage.

The visiting priest turned to greet Angelica and said, "You must be Angelica!"

She was looking into the warmest brown eyes she had ever seen. A handsome face with a beard and a very quick and easy smile. He was looking right at her, into her soul. Her heart skipped a beat. But then her head reminded her that he was a priest. Catholic priests do not have wives or girlfriends. They do not date. They take vows of poverty, chastity and obedience to the Church. Angelica was well aware of this.

Catching her breath and repeating to herself over and over again, "He is a priest, just say hello and move on," Angelica came to her senses.

Father Too-Handsome-to-be-a-Priest had other ideas. He kept talking and laughing and was obviously enjoying himself. So charming and so at ease. Angelica forgot her resolve to "just move on" and eagerly joined in the conversation and laughter.

Her parents calling to her brought her back to her awful reality and the dreaded negotiations her parents were having with Giovanni's family. This was made more painful, if that were even possible, by the five minutes of heaven talking to Father Too-Handsome with the Warm-Brown-Eyes. Looking at the big smiles on her parents' faces, Angelica guessed both sides were pleased with her proposed marriage, although nothing was formalized.

Angelica's next few days were spent either dreading the future with Giovanni or daydreaming about Father Warm-Brown-Eyes. She was trying to convince her parents to let her wait a few more years to marry. She could help care for her younger siblings at home, and Giovanni would have more time to save money for their life together. This was really just a delay tactic. Angelica hoped it would work, she could have two more years to herself. Two more years to be a person and not a bargaining chip.

The following Tuesday her mother baked the herbed bread that she baked only for special occasions. She wanted Angelica to take some loaves to the church for Father Umberto and his guest. This was a ruse and Angelica knew it. Her mother just wanted Father Umberto to talk to her about Giovanni. But today, Angelica didn't care. Maybe Father-with-the-Marvelous-Beard-and-Warm-Brown-Eyes would be there. Angelica hoped she could have another five minutes of heaven talking to him.

"So many years have passed since those days. I've lived my life and now I'm in the After Life. I can still feel the joy of talking to him. How easy it was to talk to him. How outgoing and cheerful and happy he was. Father Warm-Eyes was charming and intelligent. I talked and he listened as if what I had to say was important to him. What I said, what I felt, who I was, mattered. And it mattered to someone like Father Warm-Eyes," Angelica whispered to herself as if in prayer.

He was indeed there. When she delivered the bread, he suggested they go for a walk. Angelica took him to her favorite spot by the creek, which was secluded and shaded. She always felt comforted there. She would go there to think or to just get away from the needs of her family. Today she wanted to share her special place with Father Warm-Eyes.

This was to be their special place for the next few days. They would meet, eat lunch and just talk. Sometimes he would sing to her. Silly songs that he made up. Her heart would skip a beat. Butterflies had taken up permanent residence in her stomach. They never talked about the future.

"I lived for those very magical moments, in a world where arranged marriages and clerical vows did not exist. I loved who I was with him," sighed Angelica to herself. Then she laughed out loud. "I sound like a bad romance novel." But those moments were real and still very much a part of her being. Even in the After Life.

Father Magical Moments had to leave. He was returning to his home parish. He had been on a short vacation when he met Angelica.

He promised to write, and she promised to respond. They came up with a code name so no one would know a woman was writing to him: Luglio Agosto. July and August. They met at the end of July, and it was now early August. Angelica smiled as she remembered their little conspiracy. They were partners in their very own covert operation.

Although their relationship was chaste, her thoughts were not. She daydreamed that he would appear at her door and tell her he had given up the priesthood to marry her. Her heart would fill with such joy during these daydreams. This joy turned to pain when she would wake up to the reality that he was still a priest.

She had kept these thoughts from Father Warm-Brown-Eyes. She never touched him, never made a suggestive comment. She kept her feelings to herself. She had no one to talk to about the conflicted life she was living. She couldn't tell her parents or her siblings. Friends wouldn't understand. Even she didn't understand what she and this man who was a priest were doing.

Hourly she would tell herself, "Silly girl, he's a priest. This can never be. Keep these feelings to yourself. He is a priest. He is trained to listen and to be kind. Do nothing to encourage any kind of inappropriate actions. You are to marry Giovanni."

Angelica had come to realize that her fate was indeed to marry Giovanni. She had to make the most of it even though there was no intimate connection, no emotional closeness between them. Her soul had not been touched by Giovanni. She certainly wasn't looking forward to her body being touched by him.

Angelica was surprised at herself. Even right now, in the After Life, these memories still touched her very essence. She thought of her Emilio. She knew he had passed over to the After Life. She had hoped that she would see him there. She had been in the After Life for years and she had mostly seen only her family. She longed to see him, her Father Warm-Brown-Eyes.

Angelica returned to her revelry. She enjoyed reliving their magical moments. She remembered that each day seemed like an eternity to her without him. But each day also passed too quickly as each passing day brought her closer and closer to her marriage to Giovanni.

The day the first letter arrived, Angelica was in low spirits. Her parents were relentless in talking about the union or "The Merger," as Angelica called it. She was worn out from the endless discussions of financial security for the family, the social standing and her "duty." She knew "duty" included bearing children. And she knew what she had to do to have children. Dread had taken over Angelica's life.

And then heaven! The letter! She wanted to open the letter but she also wanted to just hold it. He, with the warm brown eyes and the charisma, had written to unworthy Angelica. She wanted to know what he had written. She was also afraid it wouldn't be intimate. Then she feared the letter would be intimate. She was torn between what should be and what she longed for. She slowly opened the letter, not wanting to rip the envelope. Angelica could still remember every word of that first letter.

"My dearest Angel,

Our time together means so much to me. There are no words to express how I feel. You have created a need in me I didn't know I had. I would be a fool not to be in love with you. I will be back in three weeks. I need to see you. Please.

Brown Eyes"

Those words, *I would be a fool not to be in love with you*, were etched in Angelica's heart. They were etched on her soul. The very essence of her being was filled with those words. "I would be a fool not to be in love with you." She could hardly breathe. What did that mean? Where could this relationship possibly go? How would she respond? She was elated, he loved her! She was worried, he loved her. She was fearful of pursuing something that could never be. But her next breath would find her filled with bliss and happy anticipation. She was so eager to see him again and yet she dreaded to see him again. He was a priest. He belonged to God, not to her. The guilt was starting to spread from her mind to her heart to her soul to her essence. And so was the desire to hold him, to touch him, to be with him. Angelica was filled with equal portions of guilt and desire, remorse and happiness. She was in love with a priest.

Sitting in the After Life, with that life behind her, reminiscing about those conflict-filled days, Angelica felt a sort of melancholy about what could have been. How different their lives would have been if he had been a free man. She had never told anyone the whole story. Not because she was ashamed. She simply didn't have anyone to tell. Not talking to anyone other than Father Handsome about their love had become her way of life. Not talking about her feelings became her life.

She was incredibly surprised by her next thought and

subsequent decision. She was going to tell Rosa the truth.

She wasn't sure how to tell her, she just knew she had to tell her. Somewhere deep inside Angelica the need to tell Rosa the truth was growing and demanding attention. Too many secrets for too long. The time had come to remove the wall between Angelica and her children. This wasn't going to be easy, but she must tell Rosa the truth. Angelica was going to tell all her children the truth. She would start with Rosa.

Talking to her mother in the After Life wasn't an unusual event for Rosa now. They had worked through their feelings about "The Story." So, she wasn't surprised when her mother said she wanted to talk to her. However, she was very surprised to see the concern on her mother's face. This is the After Life and there weren't a whole lot of concerns there. "Something's up," thought Rosa.

Angelica reached for Rosa's hand, held it and said, "Daughter, I need to tell you a story. I want to tell you a story."

She started at the beginning. Angelica explained how she met Father Handsome, the special place by the creek and the letters.

Rosa listened to her mother with interest, all the while wondering what does this have to do with me and who is this priest?

"Did he return? Did you see him?"

"Yes, Rosa, he returned. We confessed our love for one another. Both of us were experiencing joy and guilt in the same heartbeat. Each was tortured. He had made a vow to God to remain chaste and obedient to God. We were the best versions of ourselves when we were together. He told me he was becoming more caring toward his parishioners. He channeled the love he felt for me to them. We had a connectedness that went far beyond the physical. We had a deeper, more spiritual intimacy. I know that may sound trite or sound like something you would read in a book, but it was true. He had to return to his parish, he couldn't stay. Our time together had passed too quickly. He tried to kiss me goodbye, but I refused his advances.

"There were more visits, more advances and more refusals. The letters continued. Every time I wrote a letter, I planned to tell him that it was over. We could only be friends. But then I would read his tender words and I could not bring myself to do it. So, each letter became an impassioned love letter instead of a rational we-must-only-be-friends letter. I now know he struggled with this too. He would be in his parish, and he would feel his vocation so strongly. He would be so fulfilled in what he was doing. A letter from me would arrive, he would think 'no, I cannot read this, I should not read this,' yet he could not stop himself from ripping open the letter. He read my passionate letters so filled with love and devotion to him. He would start to write back we can only be friends, or he was going to stay there and never return. But he couldn't do it.

"He told me how torn he was and how many times he thought that would be the last trip to see me. It was never the last trip. He signed each letter with, 'I can't wait to hold you so closely that not even moonlight can come between us.'" Angelica still glowed at the thought of these loving words.

"The struggle wasn't just with the letters. The struggle was daily. The pain was daily. The guilt was daily.

"Watching our priest celebrate Mass and knowing that my Dearest was doing the same thing in another town simply broke my heart. It tore me to pieces. The angst was very real but so was the love. And so was our shared tenderness and our shared desire for spiritual intimacy with one another. We were happy together. We thoroughly enjoyed each other's company. We both liked who we were when we were with each other.

"I was so confused. I was torn between the love I felt for him and my Catholic faith. Our passion for one another was real. He pushed for a relationship. My resolve finally faded.

"I remember the first time we made love—or attempted to make love. His body just wouldn't respond the way we needed it to. He was embarrassed and I was shaken. I thought this might be a sign from God that our relationship should never

69

be. Eventually, everything worked as it should. We were finally together physically, sexually, emotionally and spiritually. We were blissful while we were together. When we were apart, the guilt could be consuming."

"Mom, who is this priest and what happened? How did you ever get over him?" Rosa was trying to remember the parish priests from her childhood. There was old Father Giuseppe. He could barely walk and had some strange disease. Couldn't have been Father Giuseppe. He died and Father Luigi was sent to the parish. She didn't remember her mother being particularly close to him. There was nothing warm and charming about him.

Angelica couldn't breathe for a moment. Memories of the warmth and love she saw in his warm brown eyes flooded her heart. Tears filled her eyes. She looked at her daughter and into those same brown eyes. They just weren't as warm or as loving as Rosa's father's eyes had been.

Taking a deep breath, Angelica explained, "I became pregnant."

"Oh no, Mom!"

"The day I told my parents was one of the worst days of my life. We decided I would tell them. I didn't want him to be there to witness what I knew was going to be horrible in so many ways. It was awful. I haven't thought about this in a long time. At first, they were horrified that I was pregnant and not married. They asked if the baby was Giovanni's. This could work to their advantage, as it would certainly seal the 'Merger.' They suggested we move up the wedding date. They even offered to tell people Giovanni and I were so in love we couldn't wait. So enthralled with one another that we wanted to be married as soon as possible.

"When I told them who the father was, they were shocked, dumbfounded. Speechless. Then they were furious. Didn't I know I was going to hell for having a sexual relationship with a priest? They added that we were all going to hell. They insisted upon referring to him as 'Father' as if to rub in the fact he was a priest. I had ruined them. I had selfishly ruined all their plans for a secure financial future. Talking to them was useless. They refused to believe that we were in love. They said I was nothing more than a one-night stand and worse.

"They kicked me out of the house right then and there. I left with nothing but the clothes on my back. I wasn't allowed to talk to my siblings or to tell them goodbye. They disowned me. They never forgave me.

"My grandparents were a lot more understanding. At first they were hesitant about accepting our love. They could see I was so torn between the happiness of being pregnant by the man I adored and the guilt of disobeying the Church and disappointing my parents. I was a mess. As time went on my grandparents were convinced of our love. They

71

accepted us and our child as their family. They helped us find a place to live and we moved in together."

"What happened to the baby and to this man you so loved?" Rosa refrained from saying "priest". She didn't want to offend her mother. Protecting her mother's feelings was new to Rosa.

"I had a beautiful baby girl. I named her Rosa. That baby is you, my dear child."

Rosa was now the one who was shocked and speechless. So much to absorb. Her father was a priest. Her mother had just called her "dear child" with a tenderness Rosa had never experienced from her mother. The two experiences at one time were almost too much to handle.

"My father was a priest." Rosa's head was spinning. She could barely speak. "What was his name? How long were you two together? What happened to him?"

Angelica wasn't ready to divulge that information yet. She needed to tell Rosa more of her story.

"People weren't aware of who he was. Only a few people knew that he was a priest, and they didn't live close by. He shaved his beard and didn't wear his collar. He stayed for about six months after you were born. Then one day he said he had to return to his hometown. I was shocked. I thought he was committed to me and our new family. I was filled with fear that he would never return. We had a huge argument. I accused him of wanting all the benefits of having a lover but none of the responsibilities. He was angry. He said he was doing all he could do but I needed to remember that he had a vocation and that although he loved me, he was still a priest. The pain of that realization was almost unbearable. I would never ask him to leave the priesthood. I would never ask him to choose between me and his vocation. He had to decide for himself that he was either a priest or he wasn't. The Pope would never grant a dispensation. If he left, he would be branded a renegade priest and be excommunicated. We were in an impossible position.

"I loved being his pretend wife and the mother of his child. I look at you and I see him. I was tortured by the thoughts that he would never return. I was comforted by the fact that I had you. The pain was almost unbearable. I waited for a letter and there were no letters. Finally, he wrote to tell me he was coming back in two weeks.

"Those were the longest two weeks of my life. I didn't know if he was coming back to end the relationship or to resume it. Was he going to tell me that he had left the priesthood and wanted to marry me? Or was he going to tell me he never wanted to see me again? And what about you? I knew he loved you, he adored you. I was a wreck for those two weeks. You were just a baby, so you don't remember. I tried so hard to not take it out on you and to be attentive to your needs, but I was dying inside."

Rosa was mesmerized by the story of her mother and father. Today was the first time Rosa felt an honest connection with her mother. Angelica had always been rather aloof. She didn't share her feelings or thoughts. She was a very straightforward person while running the house and the rental properties. You knew what was expected of you. But there was no warmth. No empathy or compassion. Today, Angelica was different. She seemed vulnerable. Rosa was honored her mother allowed her to see this vulnerability. She hated that her mother had been hurt.

"Mom, are you okay talking about this? I hear a pain in your voice that I've never heard before."

"I want you to know the story. I want you to know why I made the decisions that I made."

"Did he return? Did he at least offer to help support me?" Rosa was convinced her father had left her mother. Her mother would have been tainted and shunned by the community.

"He did return. He couldn't stay away. He loved me as much, if not more, than before. I was soon pregnant with your sister."

"What? Emilio was a priest? He is Serena's father, too? Is he the father of all your children? All ten of us? So, he left the priesthood? Why didn't you marry him?" Rosa was so very shocked and confused.

"Emilio and I came to an understanding. We developed a rather unique lifestyle. You know Emilio would be around for a while and then he would leave. He would be gone for months."

"Of course, I do. I hated it." Rosa remembered those long months waiting for him to return. Her mother was always on edge. She would say things that made Rosa think her father was never going to come back. Angelica would withdraw from her children. "You always said he was a fisherman. He was gone because he was working on a fishing boat."

"I thought that would make sense to a young child. Jobs were scarce at home. Lots of men went outside the area to look for work. Emilio was actually filling in for the other priests. He was an itinerant priest. He traveled from village to village celebrating Mass and performing the sacraments. He remained in the priesthood."

Angelica studied her daughter's face. There was disbelief, horror and bewilderment. She could certainly understand having a mixture of emotions and thoughts. Angelica had lived that way for many years. She had never felt such an urge to hold her child and to comfort her. She wanted Rosa to know that she was born out of love. All of the children were. Maybe they weren't planned as modern couples plan their children, but her children were wanted and loved.

"My dear first-born, Rosa, I know this might be difficult to understand. I loved him and he loved me. This was the best we could do. It wasn't ideal. Emilio loved having a family. He loved having children. But every time Emilio left, I feared this would be the last time I would see him. I feared the guilt would overwhelm him.

"I didn't have much time to feel guilty anymore. I had children to take care of and lies to remember. I had to keep our story simple. I could confide in no one. My grandparents remained somewhat supportive. Emilio's mother said she had raised her son to love and to be loved. She was happy he had found someone he truly loved. His mother was a delightful woman, and we got along very well. His family didn't live close by. We wrote to each other several times a year."

Angelica concluded her story with, "I chose that life. I'm not asking for your pity. I just want you to know the truth."

Compassion is easier in the After Life than it is in the Land of the Living. But just like in the Land of the Living you must be willing to experience compassion. Rosa was ready. She allowed herself to be filled with an understanding of the sacrifices her mother had made to share her life with the man she loved, to bear his children regardless of the cost. Her mother's behavior, her guarded feelings, now made sense. Telling Rosa couldn't have been easy for Angelica. She respected her mother's courage.

"Your father and I decided we wanted you children to go to America. There were several reasons for this decision. We'd always told you the reason was to have a better life. We wanted you and your sisters to marry a family man with a good job. We didn't want any of you to worry about money or have to skimp and do without. We wanted you to have beautiful things in a house that you owned. Your father and I wanted that for all our children. That's one reason why we wanted you to emigrate.

"But the real reason we insisted you leave was our fear. We were fearful that one of you would discover the truth about your father and his 'other life.' We needed to protect you from the decisions we had made about our relationship. We didn't want you and your brothers and sisters to be shunned. We knew no one would accept our relationship. Your father and I knew it was just a matter of time before one of you would discover the truth. You were growing up. Who knew where the future would take you or what you might discover? We were determined to spare you our anguish, our pain and our guilt. We wanted you and your siblings to have open and honest relationships. Not a relationship where you had to live a lie every day.

"I never wanted you or your brothers and sisters to live with this kind of conflict. We wanted our children to go to America to escape the prison we had made for ourselves.

"I decided to emigrate, too. Leaving Emilio to go to America was the hardest thing I've ever done other than putting you on that ship when you were only 13 years old. I thought my heart would break." Angelica had tears in her voice. She could barely speak those words. Her heart was breaking all over again.

"Wait a minute! I thought you wanted me to go to America. I thought you wanted me out of the house. I thought you were happy to see me go. You didn't cry. You didn't even seem sad that I was leaving. We didn't know if we would ever see each other again. I was 13 and you were sending me away. I thought you were heartless. And now you're telling me that you thought your heart would break?"

Catching her breath and wiping her tears, Angelica responded, "I didn't want you to know how heartbroken I was. I needed to be strong or otherwise I could never let you go. I could never have put you on that ship. I wanted a better life for you. I had to look out for your future. I had to force myself to focus on your future. That is what I kept in my head and in my heart. A future for you, free of your father's true identity. A future filled with all the happy things and the good things I thought and prayed you would find in America."

Rosa's heart and soul were touched by her mother's words. For years and years, she thought her mother had been heartless and cruel. Angelica had sent a 13-year-old girl by herself on a journey that lasted almost thirty days, to a country where she didn't speak the language or know the customs. Rosa was sent to an aunt she barely knew, an aunt who would find her a husband. The very thing that Angelica didn't want for herself. Rosa was expected to marry a man she didn't know and didn't love. She then had to move to a large city. She missed her small town. This was a difficult time for Rosa. And that was just the beginning of Rosa's life in America.

Her mother's confession of this heart wrenching departure made Rosa weep from a depth in her being she didn't know she had. Her long held resentment toward her mother had been buried so deep. This confession went to that buried but not forgotten place. They had reached another pivotal point in their relationship and healing journey.

Mother and daughter just sat there in a reflective silence for a while. Rosa would quietly weep while Angelica held her. Rosa couldn't remember a time when her mother was this compassionate or affectionate. This level of sharing emotions was new for both of them. These were two strong women who never allowed themselves to show their vulnerability to anyone. Neither one of them knew what to say. This closeness was new. It felt good.

Angelica finally broke the silence with a chuckle and said, "The After Life! I thought it would be endless days of eating dessert for breakfast, lunch and dinner. Filled with only magical moments."

"This has been magical, Mom."

Chapter Twelve

Rosa was puzzled. Her parents had created this prison for themselves in Italy by living a double life. Why didn't they both emigrate to America? In America they wouldn't have to fear being discovered. They could show their love and their affection publicly. They would be free.

She was going to see her mom again today. She'd ask her. Rosa was comfortable talking to her now. She was eager to hear more about her father.

"Why didn't Dad emigrate?"

"As you know, Emilio was a little older than I. I could see the sadness that lived in his soul and was reflected in his eyes. I thought this sadness came from living a double life. I had a sense it was becoming increasingly hard for him to live this divided life. He was less affectionate. His embraces were less passionate. He seemed distracted. We were more like brother and sister. I guessed the double life had taken its toll. I tried numerous times to talk to him. He always said nothing was wrong. But actions speak louder than words. I knew something was wrong. I thought maybe he had found someone else. I couldn't ask him that question. We had 10 children together. I knew he loved me. I also knew I had to let him go."

There were tears streaming down Angelica's face. Tears she had never cried before. Tears for the heartbreak of leaving her Father Warm-Brown-Eyes.

Pain together, torture apart. She had to choose her torture so he could be free of his pain.

"I finally decided I would go to America. We would both have fresh starts. I think that is called a geographical cure. Maybe I could leave the torture of our separation behind. I told him I was going to America and taking the children with me. We couldn't afford to send all the children at one time. You were well established. I wanted to send your sisters and your brothers. After much soul searching and many tears, we came up with a plan. My grandparents had died. I inherited some money. We used that to buy tickets for some of your siblings. We sold our farm. We used that money for the rest of the children and me. The remainder of the money was used to start our new lives.

"I did leave three children with Emilio for a short period of time. I arrived before they did so I could set up a home for them. That seemed logical to us. I never dreamed our plan would be misconstrued—that anyone would think I was a bad mother for leaving her children with their father."

Rosa felt horrible for thinking the worst of her mother. Rosa should have talked to her mom about her decision to emigrate when they were in the Land of the Living. But that just wasn't their relationship. They didn't know the other person was in pain. They just didn't know each other. There had been well maintained walls between them and lines that were never crossed. The lines were so deep they became trenches. That's just the way it was in the Land of the Living and in the After Life until just recently.

"What happened to Dad? You told me he didn't emigrate because he had died." What really happened to her father? Had her mother lied?

"I had to tell you he died because telling you the truth would involve telling you our Big Secret. Your father, my dear sweet Emilio, went back to one of his parishes and remained there. He served his parish and the community as a priest. I could not stay in touch with him. I wrote one letter to tell him that we arrived safely. I told him that our children were doing well. Staying in touch with your father would have only prolonged our pain. I simply didn't answer his letters. He only wrote twice. We knew we had to let each other go. He died about eight years after we moved to America. I have thought of him every day. I have missed him every day. I see so much of him in you and your brothers and sisters.

"Rosa, I loved him with every fiber of my being. I don't regret my actions or my passion for him and certainly I don't regret having his children, our children."

Angelica was bathed in a sense of relief. Finally telling someone the whole truth. She was astounded at Rosa's reaction. Angelica was so touched by her daughter's support and understanding. She was relieved that Rosa wasn't angry or bitter. Angelica liked this new vulnerable side of herself. The vulnerability was freeing. Angelica hadn't realized how "unfree" she had been. She had made an emotional prison for herself. She now had an unfamiliar longing to be out of this prison. Telling Rosa helped commute her self-imposed prison sentence.

Rosa looked at her mother with a new sense of appreciation. Rosa had never understood her mother. Angelica had never confided in Rosa. Angelica had always remained closed off emotionally to everyone except Emilio. Rosa did remember how excited and happy her mother would be when Emilio finally returned from his "fishing" job. She seemed so relieved. Rosa thought it was just because her mom would have some help with the farm and their growing family. Emilio had provided the heavy lifting on the farm.

Rosa wasn't sure what to do with these new feelings of appreciation and affection toward her mother. There was a sense of understanding, compassion and closeness that Rosa had never felt toward her mother. She liked it. She was grateful. The After Life was pretty amazing. She was healing. She could see herself and others in a new and positive light.

"Are you going to tell my brothers and sisters?"

"Yes, of course. I do have a favor to ask of you. Rosa, will you be there with me when I tell them?"

There was no place Rosa would rather be. Her mother had earned her respect. Angelica deserved Rosa's support.

Chapter Thirteen

Angelica was oddly calm. She felt a sense of renewed spirit. Her fear was gone as she prepared to meet the ten children she shared with Emilio. Today was the day she was telling them the true story about who their father really was. They knew Emilio as their dad, the part-time fisherman and part-time farm owner. Today she would tell them he was a priest. Her willingness to tell the truth was a surprise to her. She was accustomed to sheltering them from the truth. More accurately, she was accustomed to sheltering herself from her truth and her judgment of herself. Freedom from this judgment and the burden of lying was exhilarating. She was ready.

She was further bolstered by her eldest daughter's support. Rosa was sitting next to her to lend encouragement. Mother and daughter were forging new ground. They actively sought each other's company now. Their talks were more frequent and earnest. Both women were enjoying the new-found closeness. The walls were coming down slowly, but they were coming down.

The reunion of the ten siblings was filled with happiness and curiosity. They were happy to be together again. Although they were all in the After Life, they didn't see each other very often. They were busy with their own immediate families and their own journeys to wholeness. They were also curious why their mother had called them together. They looked at Angelica expectantly as she began to speak.

She spoke from her heart as she recounted the story about her relationship with their father, Emilio. The After Life provided an atmosphere of safety for sharing honest and sincere thoughts and feelings.

Telling the truth was essential for spiritual growth. Acceptance of the truth was not guaranteed. Acceptance was based on each person's place in her or his journey to wholeness.

The older children remembered the father they had loved. He was a disciplinarian, but he also knew how to have fun with his children. They would go on picnics and swim in the creek on Sundays after Mass. They felt loved. They knew their parents passionately loved one another. Although the three youngest really didn't know him or remember him, he was still their biological father. They had the right to know the truth, too.

There were lots of questions. Angelica answered each one honestly and completely without judgment. Angelica no longer judged herself. When she stopped judging herself, she no longer had the need or the desire to judge others. When she stopped criticizing herself, she no longer saw the faults in others. As her strong sense of self developed, she saw the wholeness in others. She was grateful for these gifts. She was grateful for the After Life and its many mercies and graces. She was honored to share them with her children and hoped for their understanding and forgiveness. But she did not expect it and would continue to love them even if they could not forgive her.

During the next few days, there were tears, more questions, more tears and eventually each child, in his or her own time, accepted the truth without recrimination. Angelica's vulnerability, her heartfelt honesty and inner peace shone brightly. The feeling of Grace was palpable when the children were with their mother. Healing was taking place. They felt an authentic closeness, an intimacy they had not experienced before. This was a glorious time!

Her mother's transformation was not lost on Rosa. She deeply respected her mother's courage and was inspired by her mother. Could Rosa use this inspiration to free herself? Rosa thought, "I'd like to tell Mom the truth about my life now. But I don't know if I'm ready. I want to live in this bliss a while longer. I don't want to upset or disappoint her. We've come such a long way. I don't want to ruin anything," Rosa thought to herself.

Rosa needed more faith in the healing process. She needed more faith in her mother and most importantly she needed more faith in herself. She recognized the need to forgive herself. She said aloud, as if it were a prayer, "There is so much to forgive, I'm not sure where to start. I could use some help, please."

Thankfully, she was about to receive this help from the Land of the Living.

Chapter Fourteen

"Our DNA results are in!" I was so excited I was dancing. My husband had taken the test, too. He was excited, but he managed not to dance. He is of Eastern European Jewish descent, 100%. No big surprises, but some clarity.

We studied my results together. We were a little amazed that I was not Scots-Irish as I thought my dad had said. I was more German and Scottish. That was Dad's contribution. As expected, I had a high percentage of Italian from my mom. The results help prove the accuracy of my research. I also had a greater sense of knowing where my roots were. This knowledge provided another connection to the "great-grands" as I liked to call my 2X, 3X, 4X, etc., great-grandparents. We were pleased with the DNA test.

Very simply put, our DNA tests will show how much DNA we share with a relative. How much we share is determined by centimorgans. Centimorgans are a unit of measuring genetic linkage. It is abbreviated as cM. The more cMs you have with another person, the more closely related you are. Siblings have a higher number of cMs than cousins will have. These genetic measurements are used to help determine first cousins, second cousins and on down the genetic ladder.

Using this little bit of knowledge, we moved on to looking for possible cousins. I recognized some of the names of people I had met online who were related via my grandmother's siblings. I had a great time looking at all the results. I compared DNA profiles with several "new to me" people to determine how we were related. I was constantly on the hunt for more information and always ready to meet a new cousin.

So many of these new cousins were from my grandmother's family. She had so many sisters and brothers. Lots of new cousins. And there were my first cousins, Diana, Elaine and her brother Andrew. We knew we were cousins, so I didn't really look at those results—until Elaine called.

"Did you notice that none of the possible cousins are from our grandfather's side of the family? There are no Amoratis, just Casertas. Shouldn't there be people who are from our grandfather's side of the family? Didn't he have sisters and brothers?" Elaine was brilliant in her observation. I had overlooked it.

"Information about Antonio is scarce. We know his mother's name, Domenica Amorati. Her maiden name was Bruno. I think Antonio had a brother, Pasquale. There is a Pasquale Amorati listed as my mother's godfather. I saw it on her baptismal record, although she never mentioned him. I'm guessing he was Antonio's brother. That is all we know of his family. I have searched and searched for more. I can't even verify that Pasquale was indeed his brother. I can't find immigration information for Antonio or Pasquale. Diana doesn't know if he had siblings, either. Maybe no one in the Amorati family has taken DNA tests."

That seemed unlikely to both of us. I was staring at the results on my computer screen. I noticed my first cousin on my dad's side, Ellen, had taken the test, too. Weird thing, she had so many more cM markers, genetic markers, than Elaine and I had. Ellen and I had 1200 plus. Elaine and I had only 429. I pointed that out to Elaine.

"That's odd. I wonder what that means? I have more cMs with my first cousin from my mom's side than I have with you, too," said Elaine.

"We need to look into this. We need more information. I'll call you when I know more." I had offered to research our findings.

I started looking online for more information about DNA results and what the results can indicate. I studied the information. I even showed it to my husband. He agreed with me. "Elaine, Andrew, Diana and I are half-first cousins. That means we have different grandfathers. Grandmother Rosa must have had a few affairs? My grandfather is not Antonio Amorati. I don't think he is Elaine's grandfather either. I'm not sure about Diana. Elaine will be shocked."

Chapter Fifteen

"Mom! Mom!" shouted Rosa to Angelica. Rosa was disturbing her mother's mid-afternoon nap in the After Life. Mother and daughter had been enjoying their close relationship since she had told Rosa the truth about her father, Emilio. The After Life provided the time both women needed to find themselves and their truth. They were finding the strength in the After Life to confront their fears. These fears had paralyzed them when they were in the Land of the Living. Their fears had been obscured by judgments and self-absorption. They were realizing this now. As they were healing, their relationship became mutually empowering.

Angelica was experiencing an inner peace that allowed her to see others as they truly are, children of God, an extension of God. Rosa was still working on her fears and self-judgment. She was making progress, but there was more progress to be made. There were more fabrications to face.

"She's at it again," wailed Rosa.

"Who's at what again?" Angelica was pleased that her daughter would turn to her in her time of obvious need. This would not have happened before—in either the Land of the Living or the After Life. Her daughter's needs were important to her. Angelica loved this new feeling she had toward her daughter. Compassion, she thought it must be.

"That, that great-granddaughter of yours. Emma. You know, my little Lucia's daughter, Emma." Rosa was clearly agitated.

"Oh, yes! She is the one who outed you and your tall tale about your supposed father, Andrea Diserta. What else could she possibly have found? And how is she finding out all of this?"

"Outed me? Outed? Where do you get these words?"

"People who have passed over recently. They talk, I listen. They use words and expressions I've never heard before. It is fascinating. I have a whole new vocabulary. Go on, Rosa. I want the scoop. I want the 411." Angelica loved using her new vocabulary, especially with Rosa. She wanted to lighten the mood.

"I told you before she is using that computer machine thing. Now they have some test that will tell you your ethnicity. I don't care about that. But this test will somehow connect you to other relatives. It determines if you are first or second cousins. I don't understand how, I just know it does. Everything is unraveling. EVERYTHING. I hate that computer thingy. This is the worst!"

Rosa was genuinely horrified at what could possibly happen with these new discoveries. Emma and Elaine. Couldn't they just be happy knowing they are related? Do they have to analyze every little thing?

"Rosa, dear child, start from the beginning. Why are you so worried? What is upsetting you? Obviously,

94

Emma knows she is part Italian. Both of her mother's parents are from Italy. She knows who her cousins are. She grew up with them. Her sister, Marianne, has told me stories about their trips to Pittsburgh to visit their cousins. What could be the problem?" Although Angelica was sincerely concerned about what was upsetting her daughter, she didn't understand the issue. Understanding and being there for her daughter had become essential to Angelica. She just wasn't sure how to "be there."

Rosa took several deep breaths trying to calm down. She looked at her mother. This woman had been impossible to talk to when Rosa was in the Land of the Living. Rosa would never have divulged such information to her. She would never have allowed herself to be vulnerable in front of such a formidable person. Even if that person was her mother. However, their relationship had expanded and grown. Gone was the judgment. Gone was the coldness and distance. Her lifelong anger toward her mother was losing its power over her. Her mother's confession was a healing balm for both of them. She felt confident she could tell her mother the story, the whole story, and there would be no recriminations. She knew her mother would help her. She just had to help her.

"Elaine and Emma have made a discovery that I hoped no one ever would make. Mom, they have discovered they are only half-first cousins." Rosa said this very slowly and thoughtfully.

"What does that mean? What is the significance of that?"

"They are only half-first cousins because they have different grandfathers."

Rosa let that revelation soak in for a couple of moments.

"Different grandfathers? What do you mean, different grandfathers? Antonio is their grandfather."

Rosa wanted to be unburdened from the lie she had lived with since she was 17 years old.

"Do you remember how everyone would comment that Gianna and Minnie looked like each other, but they didn't look like anyone else in the family? That is because Antonio is not their father."

"Rosa—start at the beginning, please. Is Antonio the father of Antonia?"

"Antonio is her father." Rosa responded as if reliving a painful experience. "I was 14 years old and married to a man-child. He was 19. We were just kids who barely knew what we were doing either in or out of bed. I didn't know anything about men. I wasn't allowed to learn to read or write Italian because you and Dad thought I would use it to write letters to boys. I knew nothing of the world when I left home for America. I knew even less about men and marriage."

"What about Carlo in Italy? I thought you two were having sex." Angelica remembered how angry and disappointed she had been in her daughter. She was supposed to save herself for marriage. This would have made matchmaking easier for her. Rosa had risked everything by being with Carlo.

"Oh, Mom! I made all of that up. I never touched him. He never touched me. I made it up to make you angry. I told all those lies because I wanted your attention. I was a virgin when I married Antonio."

"Well! You certainly got my attention. I thought your father was going to explode. He never liked Carlo. He thought he was a pompous jerk who would never amount to anything. And he never did. I'm more concerned that you didn't think you had my attention. You did. I just wasn't good at showing it. You understand now why I seemed detached." Angelica was referring to the story about Rosa's father, Emilio.

The two women had had a rocky mother-daughter relationship for so long. They were both grateful for this new compassionate understanding between the two of them. There had been too many missed opportunities for a healthy relationship. Angelica had been so wrapped up in her fears about her relationship with Emilio, that she didn't have time for her daughter. Rosa had been left on her own from a young age.

Angelica chortled, "I always wondered what you saw in Carlo. How could you, why would you have sex with him?"

"Mother, really!"

The lightened mood helped Rosa to relax. She had details to tell her mother that were painful to relive.

Rosa didn't know where to start. She had become an expert at hiding the truth. She was quite adept at keeping her lies straight. This was the first time she felt safe enough to tell anyone the truth.

"I'll start with the day you and Dad told me I was going to America. I was very excited because I thought all of us were going together—as a family. I knew I could face the journey and a new country if I were with my family. I thought finally we would be like other families. Dad wouldn't be gone for months at a time. You wouldn't be so worried because he would be home with us. I hated his absences. All of us seem to wither when he was away. We would only come back to life when he returned. I had pictured us as a close-knit family in America."

Angelica was pained by her daughter's recollection of her childhood. She knew what Rosa was saying was true.

"When I realized I was going by myself, I was terrified." Rosa felt a lump in her throat and tears rising in her voice.

"You didn't act terrified. I thought you were excited. You were going on an adventure to meet your wealthy prince."

"Mom, I didn't care about a prince, I wanted a family to love and support me. I wanted a family who would

show me that love and support. I wanted stability."
Rosa was amazed she had blurted that out to her
mother. She would never have said that to her mother
in the Land of the Living.

"Oh, my dear Rosa, I am so sorry. I didn't know. I wish
I had been more present to you—more available."
Rosa could hear the earnestness in her mother's voice.

"The day I boarded that ship was the most terrifying
day of my life. I thought I could make a deal with you. I
almost—almost—offered to become a nun—to spend
my life in prayer for you and Dad. I thought maybe
then you would be happy with me. Maybe then you
would approve of me." Tears were flowing down
Rosa's cheeks. "I would have done almost anything to
stay at home, in Italy, with my family."

Mother and daughter sat in silence as Rosa collected
her thoughts. That period in Rosa's life was filled with
uncertainty and aloneness. She had pushed those
thoughts and feelings away until they were deeply
hidden. Exposing them today, with her mother and
not *at* her mother, felt freeing. She could finally
breathe.

"The journey itself wasn't too bad. The view of the
ocean was beautiful and a little intimidating. Traveling
with a couple of neighbors made it easier. We arrived
in America. I thought we would never finish the
entrance questions. Finally, I was on my way to Ohio.
We went by train. Aunt Louisa met us at the station.
Her English seemed flawless to me. She was kind and

welcoming. She helped our two friends from home find their way to their next destination. Then we went to her house. Aunt Louisa already had someone in mind for me. His name was Antonio Giuseppe Amorati."

Angelica thought about her older sister, Louisa. She had been the first to emigrate to America. She thought Louisa was so brave. She had married for love, yet she was known as a matchmaker. She arranged marriages—not love matches. Angelica appreciated Louisa's help in finding a match for Rosa. Angelica was determined that Rosa's husband be selected for her so she wouldn't be tempted as Angelica had been. Antonio was 19 and from a good southern Italian family. They owned a small farm which more than adequately provided for their financial needs. Angelica thought this was a good match. She wasn't going to leave anything to chance. She wanted Rosa to have a stable income and own her own house. Above all, she wanted Rosa to be married and have children.

Rosa continued her story, "Antonio was gregarious, a people person who didn't want to be a farmer in America. He thought the future was in transportation. In railroads, to be exact. His desire to be a part of the railroad industry led us to Pittsburgh, Pennsylvania. He had secured a good paying job with the railroad. He would be gone Monday through Friday. I would be on my own while he was gone.

Antonio wanted to start a family right away. He was in a big hurry to have children."

"You wanted children, didn't you, Rosa? You had experience with babies. You helped me with your sisters and brothers."

"I was 14 years old! I was inexperienced sexually. I didn't know what to expect from him or from marriage. I wanted time to adjust. I could barely speak English. I was in an unfamiliar country. I didn't know anyone. The city was so big, so many people. I was grateful we moved to an Italian neighborhood. That helped, but life was tough—really tough." Rosa sighed, remembering the sense of isolation and confusion.

"I didn't understand Antonio. He was in such a rush to have children. He didn't seem to enjoy sex. He wasn't tender. He didn't understand how inexperienced I was in the bedroom." This was a painful conversation for Rosa because it was so personal. She was not in the habit of revealing such intimate details. She had never confided any of this to anyone. There wasn't anyone to share her fears and confusion with. She had been alone in her confusion and pain. Rosa was surprised she was telling her mother. Somehow, sharing her past with her mother helped ease the pain.

"Then I had two children who died when they were babies. I was brokenhearted." Rosa brushed away a tear. Angelica could feel her daughter's sorrow.

Rosa took a deep breath. Her words kept coming. She had so much to tell her mother. "Antonio's response to the loss of the babies was to drink. I thought Antonio drank too much before they died. After their deaths he drank more and more often. He would get so angry at me. I never understood what I had done to make him so angry. He would complain about my cooking or housekeeping. Most of the time he was just angry. He was a combination of melancholy and anger. He would be happy when he invited his friends to the house. When they were around, he could be fun. Nobody could play the accordion like Antonio! His friends, mostly men, would sing and dance. I liked having other people around. I didn't mind the extra work I had to do or the extra money it cost. His friends were a buffer between me and his anger. I felt alone or lost when there were just the two of us together. We didn't have much to talk about. I was alone when he was gone during the week, and I felt lonely when he was home for the weekend."

"Oh, Rosa, you're breaking my heart. I wish you would have told me. I wish I could have helped you." Angelica was appalled at Antonio's behavior. Her heart ached for her daughter.

"Antonio occasionally seemed to regret his cruel words, but he didn't stop. I remember when I was pregnant with Antonia. He thought I was lazy. The truth is I was having a difficult pregnancy. I was sixteen and pregnant for the third time. My body needed rest. He couldn't or wouldn't understand this.

There would be months between his outbursts. I would think he had stopped. Then something would trigger the anger and he would lash out at me. I'm telling you all of this because I would like you to try to understand my life and the decisions I made."

"I don't think you need to justify your actions to me, Rosa. I'm sorry you were abused. I'm sorry you were unhappy." Angelica was sincere. She was realizing for the first time how much she loved her daughter and how much she had let her down.

"There is more to the story, Mom." Rosa wanted to tell the whole truth about her life with Antonio. Sharing this with her mother had never felt more important. Letting go of the need to hide her life and her pain was liberating. Hearing herself tell her own story helped to put things into perspective. This helped Rosa to heal.

"I'm here. I'm honored that you will share this with me. Tell me whatever you want to when you are ready." There was no sense of judgment, only support.

"Antonia was about two years old. I was taking her for a walk through the neighborhood to the little park by St. Stephen's Church. I had been so busy with housework, I had barely combed my hair. I was wearing a plain housedress that I wore to clean the house. Antonia was fussy and I needed some fresh air. I tried to stay busy all the time so I wouldn't think about how miserable I was. I did find joy in being with Antonia. I enjoyed the walks because I would occasionally talk to someone. Remember all our neighbors were Italian so there was no language barrier. We arrived at the park in time to listen to a street musician and a singer. Antonia was enthralled and wasn't fussing. I was enjoying the music. The singer was a very handsome Italian man, with a sleek body, thick black hair, dark eyes and a gorgeous smile. He was certainly fun to look at!"

"Did you know him from the neighborhood?"

"I don't remember seeing him before that day. When they finished their impromptu performance, he walked over to me. He smiled that smile. What a smile! We started talking. The conversation was easy and lighthearted. He seemed so happy. Such a contrast to Antonio. I remember Antonia started to fuss again. He picked her up and sang a silly little made up song to her. She was all smiles and giggles."

"Did Antonio sing to Antonia?" Angelica was searching for some redeeming value in Antonio.

"No, not really. He would hold her for a few minutes and then hand her back to me. He thought she was my responsibility. He did like her to wear pretty clothes. I know he loved her, but he didn't know how to show his love."

"Tell me more about this singer. I'm guessing you saw him again?"

"I did. I started taking Antonia out daily, at the same time. He would be waiting in the park. I started to dream about his smile. He looked at me so differently than Antonio. He told me how pretty he thought I was the first time he saw me. Me. With uncombed hair and an old house dress. Pretty. I will admit to combing my hair and wearing something nicer after that. A man had never told me I was pretty. Antonio had never looked at me like that."

"Antonio never complimented you? Never told you that you were pretty?"

"No, Antonio always complained if I wasn't dressed up and my hair perfect. He was always so perfectly groomed. He expected me and the children to look perfect, too."

"You are beautiful, Rosa, I can't believe Antonio didn't see that. I didn't mean to interrupt—go on with your story, please."

"We met for about four weeks in the park. The weekends were long and lonely with Antonio. I looked forward to Mondays so I could see Gianni. I dreaded Fridays. During this time with Gianni, I felt better about myself. I took more care with my appearance. I had such fun with him! Our laughter was like therapy for me. I felt lighter and more alive than I had in years. I actually started thinking maybe I could have a happy life. I dreamed about what my life could be with Gianni. A life filled with our laughter, our talks and our closeness.

"He had a small efficiency apartment he shared with his younger brother. His family owned a grocery store that was quite successful. He worked there and sang on the side. His passion was singing. Such a gorgeous voice.

"He finally asked me if he could see me alone. I was in heaven. I hated sex with Antonio and would avoid it. But oh, Gianni. I had strong urgings for him. I wanted to be alone with him and to share his bed. I had some feelings of guilt about Antonio. But there was no love there. I knew he didn't love me. We were married because we were too young and inexperienced to think we could say no to the arranged marriage. We thought we had to do what our families told us to do. Our desires were not a consideration. I had found some happiness with Gianni. I happily let him and his marvelous smile into my life.

"And he happily welcomed me into his bed. I finally discovered what the big deal was about sex! He was gentle and loving. Such passion between the two of us, I had never experienced anything close to that with Antonio. I lived for the moments we could be together. My heart was overflowing with love and desire for him. I hated the weekends. I had to be home with Antonio when I was in love with another man.

"My Fridays were filled with ugly thoughts about Antonio and his approaching return. I had what I called a 'litany' of things I didn't like about him. Some of the things on the list were unimportant. Putting them on that list made them important and gave them power. His tidiness and fastidious grooming were annoying. I had a small child at home who constantly needed my attention. Children aren't neat and tidy. They spill things. They are messy. They are children, not mini-adults. He held me accountable for the stains on my apron. Ridiculous. I added that to my 'litany.' It gave me permission to do what I did."

"Oh, Rosa! What did you do? Did Antonio ever find out about Gianni?"

"We loved each other deeply. We continued to see each other for the next several months. I was in heaven and hell. Heaven with him and hell without him. He was in his own hell, too. His family must have heard something about us. They suddenly insisted that he marry the girl they had long ago selected for him. I've never said her name. I won't say it. He told me his parents' decision on a Friday afternoon. That was our last time together before his marriage. The following Monday I found out I was pregnant. I knew it was his baby. Antonio hadn't touched me since I had been pregnant with Antonia. I was fine with Antonio leaving me alone in the bedroom, but now I was pregnant."

"What did you tell Antonio? What did you do?"

"When Antonio came home Friday night, I was dressed up, my hair was perfect, the house was perfect. I fixed his favorite food. I splurged on wine. I put Antonia to bed early. I tried to seduce him. I knew more about sex now, so I thought I could do this. I didn't want to sleep with him, but I was pregnant with Gianni's baby. I had to do something, even though I couldn't stand the thought of Antonio touching me. But the seduction failed. He pretty much laughed in my face. He said he couldn't stand touching *me*. He hated sex with me. He was so unhappy being married to me. He had sex with me because he knew having babies was expected of him. He was only doing his 'duty.' He didn't want to have anything to do with me sexually. I was hurt, yet relieved. I felt the same way about him. But I was still pregnant with another man's baby."

Angelica felt responsible for her daughter's predicament. She had insisted that Louisa arrange a marriage for Rosa. Maybe she should have let Rosa find a husband on her own. "I'm so sorry, Rosa," was all Angelica could murmur.

"The next part will surprise you. Partly out of desperation and partly to get even with him, I blurted out that I was pregnant. He said he didn't care. He was glad another man did his dirty work for him. Antonio didn't mind having more children. It made him look good. Virile, he said. He demanded that the father of the baby never know I was pregnant or had a child. The father could not know his child or have any contact with the child. I agreed. I wasn't in a position to bargain with him."

"I've got to interrupt! Antonio was glad another man did his dirty work for him? What was going on with him?"

"I didn't know then and I don't know now. I couldn't have Gianni, but I could have his child. I named her Gianna. I could look at her and see my precious Gianni, the love of my life."

"Gianna was everyone's favorite. She was so sweet, kind and loving." Angelica had always enjoyed the company of her bright and cheerful granddaughter. "I don't understand your arrangement with Antonio. I'm grateful he financially supported you and the children. With Gianni's baby, maybe you could have a little happiness inside that cold and abusive marriage."

"Mom, do you remember the day you were at my house after Gianna was born? You saw me put away a small box in the cupboard in the kitchen."

"I think I saw you *hide* a box!"

"You're right. I was hiding it. I had a small photo—one of those postcard photos of Gianni. He gave it to me so I could hold him close when he wasn't with me. I treasured that photo to the day I passed over.

"Antonio seemed to lighten up after Gianna's birth—like a burden had been lifted from his shoulders. He was hoping for a promotion at work. Do you remember that we lied about Antonia's birthdate so we could enroll her in school a year and a half early? That was his idea. He couldn't do the math required for his job. He wanted Antonia to go to school so she could help with his paperwork. The plan worked. A few years later, he was promoted. Antonia calculated the math for him. She was forced to grow up too soon."

"Rosa, that explains Gianna's birth, but what about Minnie? I thought you said they had the same father?"

"Immediately after they were married, Gianni and his wife moved to Altoona. About a year later his grandmother died. He returned for her funeral. We saw each other at church. Our passion for each other was still alive. One look was all it took for us to throw all reason and caution to the wind. I still loved him. He still loved me. We had to be together even though we knew there was no future. We spent as much time together as possible. I didn't like the sneaking around, but I loved being with him. He was there for five days. I kept my word to Antonio. Gianni left town without knowing he had a baby daughter. I soon realized I was pregnant again and was having a second child with Gianni. I was thrilled about the baby, but I was horribly depressed that I could never share this happiness with him. I longed for him to be in my life, but I knew that was impossible. I had to content myself with having his two daughters. They look so much alike. There could be no doubt that they have the same father."

"Antonio was ok with this?"

"He accepted the news with some reservation. Again, he insisted that the father not know about the child. I agreed to his demands. Antonio never knew the girls had the same father. He never knew his name."

"Gianni never knew about his two daughters?"

"Not exactly, Mom. He found out I had two more children. He wrote to me to ask if they might be his. He said he knew there must be a good reason I had hidden the news from him. I responded, explaining the arrangement I had made with Antonio. Because of Antonio's demands, I couldn't tell Gianni they were his children. I did buy new dresses for both girls and had their pictures taken. I mailed the photos to him. I told him we could not be together again, nor could he contact me or the children. I was afraid of what Antonio would do. I needed to remain married to him for the sake of the children. I needed to obey his rules. I never saw or heard from Gianni again. My heart has been in pieces since then. I don't think I ever fully recovered from losing my precious Gianni."

"I thought Antonio was good to your children. Did he treat Gianna and Minnie differently?"

"No. I have to give Antonio credit for that. He was never a hands-on dad. He didn't change diapers or feed the children, but he was never unkind toward them. He provided for our family. Antonio never mentioned their parentage to me or to them. Gianna and Minnie were very close. They had a very special bond. Sometimes I wondered if they knew they had a different father and were only half-sisters to their siblings. I couldn't ask them, of course."

"How did you explain their appearance? They look so much alike but there is no similarity with your other children."

"I usually tried to laugh it off. Who understands genetics?"

There was another reason why her children didn't resemble one another. In time, Rosa would share this other reason.

Chapter Sixteen

"I don't care if the DNA results say we are half-cousins, we are still cousins." I appreciated Elaine's heartfelt proclamation. Finding out we were half-first cousins had been a shock for both of us.

We were still trying to make sense of our DNA results. Half-cousins meant we had different grandfathers. Elaine's dear father, my Uncle Armani, was really a half-uncle. I couldn't stand the thought of that. I was losing my family. These were the people I grew up knowing and loving as aunts, uncles and cousins. I didn't know my grandfather because he died many years before I was born. I did grow up with his name and photo, though. The proud man in the photo with his six children. And now I find out he isn't the father of some of them. Is he the father of any of them?

My thoughts and feelings were all over the place. I thought about my mother. She never knew her biological father. Or did she? She was only half-sister to her beloved brother and sisters. Would this knowledge have changed anything in her life? Would she have had more choices, more opportunities if her biological father had some involvement in her life? Who was he? Did he know he had a daughter with Rosa? Was she conceived out of love? A one-night stand? What was his medical history? I needed to know that for my own health records.

Through my research, I became aware of the fabrications, misrepresentations, omissions, commissions, lies that had been told to us as if they were facts. Our family history was based on those supposed facts. I found them to be interesting and confusing. This, however, was on a different level. I had lost a whole branch of my family. The sense of loss was real. I lost part of what I thought made me, me.

There was an emptiness inside me that was formerly filled with the concept of my family headed by the mustached, accordion playing, hard drinking Antonio Giuseppe Amorati. Now, I was not an Amorati.

Who was I? Who was my family? I have a set of half family somewhere in the world. Do they know about Rosa? Do they know about my mother?

Not only was Antonio not my grandfather, but his mother, Domenica, was not my great-grandmother. The lovely picture I had in my heart of a devout, petite Italian woman praying for all of us was still lovely, but she wasn't my great-grandmother.

What was going on with Rosa? Was my grandmother lonely? In love? Lustful? Easy? I dismissed the idea of promiscuity. In my heart of hearts, I knew, I just knew, she had good reasons for her decisions, choices and actions. Would I ever know those reasons?

Elaine and I were talking on the phone two or three times a day. We were trying to come to terms with our thoughts and varying emotions. My relationship with Elaine was now more important than ever. We still had each other and Diana, and Elaine's brother Andrew. Half or whole didn't matter, I loved them.

I enjoyed researching my family and discovering the facts, and I liked the sense of connectedness. I knew where I came from and where I belonged. I came from Rosa Caserta and Antonio Amorati, and I belonged to a whole host of their children and their children's children. And now I didn't. I didn't realize how important this connectedness was until I lost a major portion of it.

"So what do we do?" asked Elaine during one of our many phone calls. "Is there more we can determine from the DNA results? Are there any answers there?"

We started comparing who her cousins were with mine. I made endless notes. I researched so many trees. All I ended up with was a list of unfamiliar names. Of course, I could contact some of these people. But what was I going to say? "Did your relative have an affair with my grandmother?"

Eventually, through the process of elimination, we found a strong possibility for Elaine. The family had lived in the Pittsburgh area when her father would have been conceived. There wasn't much information about the man who was the possible biological father of my Uncle Armani. His name was Albert, but it looks like he changed his name. He may have gone by Mani. We were encouraged by that name. Could Mani be short for Armani? Was Albert an attempt to sound more American? He was married and had a family. A couple of these family members had taken a DNA test and were a match with Elaine, but not with me or Diana. I contacted a couple of them via the website.

They weren't familiar with our family name of Caserta. We were hoping against all odds that they would have heard of the name. They didn't have more information about their relative that proved helpful to us. We didn't tell them we suspected their grandfather of having an affair with our grandmother. We had reached a dead end with Elaine's family. We hoped more people in her newly found family would take a DNA test so we could confirm the relationship.

I wondered if Grandmother Rosa would have told the truth if she had been confronted with our new knowledge?

Chapter Seventeen

Oh, did Rosa ever remember Armani! Handsome with beautiful wavy hair, he could have been part Greek and part Italian. He was well built, muscular and funny. What a good sense of humor Armani had. Not only was he full of corny jokes, but he was also brilliant. Armani could speak several languages. He spoke his native Italian, beautiful English, romantic French, Spanish, and was working on Greek.

After the disastrous ending of her love affair with Gianni, Rosa focused on her children and mending her broken heart. She was lonely. Life with Antonio was a grind. They didn't pretend to be in love or loving. They lived in the house together, but she was still alone and lonely. Antonio was good to the children. He never mentioned that he wasn't Gianna's and Minnie's father, which was a great relief to Rosa. She thought their arrangement was odd, but she was grateful he remained silent on the subject.

Her days were filled with cooking and cleaning for her children and the boarders. She still dreaded the weekends when Antonio would return home from his railroad job. She never knew what kind of mood he would be in or what fault he would find with her. Life was repetitive and bleak. Her children were the only bright lights in her life.

Getting over Gianni had been tough. She would never forget him or fall out of love with him, but Rosa was finally feeling better. The pain of losing Gianni had been pushed deep down inside. She needed to have something to look forward to. She needed to get out of the house, away from the "sameness" that had taken over her life. The "sameness"—every day the same as the day before with no relief in sight.

Shopping, maybe she would go shopping. Maybe that would help. She had left Antonia home with the babies, walked to the streetcar stop and breathed in her freedom.

Shopping was fun. She had saved some money that Antonio didn't know about. Rosa bought a beautiful blue dress and splurged on a boa-type scarf. This certainly wasn't for Antonio's benefit. Although he would compliment her when she dressed up.

Where would she wear such a dress?

The answer was staring her in the face. She saw a notice for a new club opening just outside her neighborhood. "That's it! I'll wear my new dress and boa and go to that club," Rosa said to herself. She wanted to laugh, have fun, talk to an adult. She wanted to feel alive again.

She laughed at the name of the club, Fuggiamo. Translated from the Italian, it meant "let's escape." Escape is what she longed for.

The day finally arrived. Rosa was going to Fuggiamo. She did feel a little guilty, leaving a nine-year-old with a four- and six-year-old at home, but Antonia was experienced for her young age. Besides, thought Rosa, I'll only be gone for an hour or two.

Rosa looked beautiful in her new dress—and she knew it. She felt good. She was still young—only twenty-five. She had a wonderful time meeting new people and connecting with some old acquaintances. She enjoyed the companionship and the conversations. There was plenty of laughter and flirting. She indulged in both. Going to the club became a weekly event. This was Rosa's lifeline.

The lifeline was made sweeter by catching the eye of the very handsome and intelligent Armani. He taught summer classes at the local university. He had traveled all over Europe before he immigrated. His hometown in Italy was only 50 miles from Rosa's small community. Armani was charismatic. People flocked to him, women threw themselves at him. But he had his eye on Rosa.

Armani didn't live in Pittsburgh. He was there just for a couple of months during the summer. Then he was going to travel around America for a year. Rosa was so intrigued by him.

She admired his education, the way he spoke and his nomad lifestyle. She longed to be that free. She longed to be that educated. Her own schooling was sketchy. Her parents didn't want her to attend school. She had immigrated to America when she was only 13. Rosa loved to be around people who were intelligent and well spoken. The fact that Armani was so physically alluring was a plus. They had enjoyed a harmless, fun flirtation so far.

Looking back so many years ago to that Tuesday afternoon when Rosa and Armani were finally alone, Rosa found herself smiling. She liked thinking about Armani and their time together. Fuggiamo was unusually empty that afternoon. Rosa was thrilled. She could have Armani all to herself. She had not intended to take on another lover. She had three children by two fathers. She thought that sounded scandalous. Neither guilt at breaking her wedding vows nor a sense of loyalty to her husband entered into this decision. She and Antonio were hardly husband and wife. There was no physical relationship between them. At the same time, she wanted to protect her heart. She didn't want to take a chance on falling in love again.

Armani looked particularly handsome that day. He spoke to her in French and then translated it into Italian. So romantic. Speaking Italian was much easier for Rosa, but the French was so beautiful. It wasn't long before they found themselves in each other's arms in Armani's bed. He rented a room a block from the club. Even the room fascinated Rosa. It was filled with books, papers and magazines. There was a large map of the world on the wall. Check-marked towns and cities indicated Armani's travels. There were lots of check marks. Other places were circled. These were places he planned to visit. Education and traveling were his passions.

Rosa was charmed by all things Armani. Armani did not smoke those cheap cigarettes, he smoked a pipe. He wore a stylish rag cap. Or maybe it just looked stylish on him. He wore wire rimmed glasses when he read poetry to her. Rosa was infatuated by his worldly, romantic aura. He thought she was beautiful and very desirable. Their time together was intoxicating.

Rosa lost herself in the memories of that afternoon with Armani and the numerous other afternoons they spent together. Summer classes were over. Sadly, they had to bid farewell to one another. They both knew this day was coming. They both knew they were there for a good time but not for a long time. There was never any hint of a long-term relationship or a commitment for any sort of a future. They didn't make plans to stay in touch.

A few weeks later when Rosa didn't have her period, she knew she was pregnant again. Armani was gone. She didn't have an address for him, but she didn't want to tell him. She had been infatuated with him. She enjoyed having sex with him, but there was no future with him. Anyway, it just wasn't possible. She could never divorce Antonio. She had to think of her family.

Rosa was straightforward in her approach to informing Antonio. She simply stated she was pregnant. He showed no emotion, but he did remind her of his conditions. The biological father could never see the child or be involved in the child's life. Rosa already knew this and agreed. She never saw Armani again. He never knew Rosa gave birth to a beautiful baby boy. She named him Armani after his father. Their son was the apple of Rosa's eye. He reminded her so much of her fun-loving and intelligent summer love. She wanted her son to grow up to be just like his biological father.

Years later Rosa would move heaven and earth to make sure that her son not only had a four-year college degree, but he would also earn a PhD. She encouraged him to learn several languages. She wanted him to be as well educated as his father. She wanted him to have the opportunity to learn what she never had. Rosa wanted her son to live in a world of books, classrooms and a world map with numerous checks and circles. A world she could never inhabit.

Chapter Eighteen

Telling her mother about Armani had been easier than Rosa expected. Rosa was learning to love herself and to forgive herself. She was no longer making excuses about why she did what she did. She was understanding her life and her choices, and she could see the impact her choices had on others. There was more to tell her mother. She would tell her soon, but now Rosa was enjoying time to herself. She spent her days reflecting on her life. Today she was thinking about her eighth child, Aria, and the circumstances surrounding her conception.

Rosa's day had been uneventful. Truthfully, the last couple of years had been uneventful. Rosa had four children at home. She had very little time to go to the club. Since the birth of her son Armani, Rosa stayed home. There was so much work to do with four children and the boarders. Rosa was lonely although she was never alone. She missed male attention and affection, but she wasn't sure how to fill this longing for a man's warm embrace.

Her husband, Antonio, came home every Friday at 6 PM, and by 8:00 PM he would be drunk. This Friday night was different. He was in a very good mood, having invited several friends to their home. Rosa didn't mind the extra people. She welcomed his friends. It meant she didn't have to be alone with him. The silence between the two of them was unbearable.

His friends were lively company and they liked to include Rosa in their fun. Antonio played the accordion while their friends sang and danced. He was an excellent accordion player. Sometimes he would play their piano. He was naturally musically talented. The atmosphere was filled with laughter and gaiety. Rosa even had a glass or two of wine. This was one of the rare occasions Rosa had fun at home with her husband.

After a few more songs and another glass of wine, their friends went home. As they climbed the stairs to their separate bedrooms, Antonio reached out to take Rosa's hand. He bent down and gently kissed her. They had not touched in years. They hadn't touched since he told her he couldn't stand to touch her or to make love to her. Tonight was different. He was kind and tender. Most importantly, he wasn't drunk or angry.

The next day Rosa woke up in her husband's bed. She was genuinely confused by his behavior last night. She was confused about her behavior, too. The physical closeness had felt good, but what did it mean? She hoped they would talk about it. Maybe this was a positive turning point in their relationship.

Antonio was already up and out of the house. He didn't return for hours. When he did return, he was already drunk.

They never spoke about that night. However, Rosa had a beautiful reminder, a daughter. A stunning baby girl with jet black hair and very dark eyes. She was the beauty of the family. They named her Aria Domenica. Aria in honor of his love of music, and Domenica after his mother.

Aria was the combination of her father's gregariousness and Rosa's beauty. She inherited her father's love of music and his natural music ability. She also had his theatrical flair. Father and daughter were very close. He taught her to play the piano and they would sing together. He wanted her to learn to play the accordion, but she thought it was too old fashioned. He just laughed. Aria could do no wrong in his eyes. To Antonio's credit, he tried not to show favoritism. But anyone watching the father-daughter duo could see they were each other's favorite. Two talented peas in a musical pod.

Their special bond ended abruptly when Antonio started complaining about his stomach. This was 1925. Doctors prescribed medication and cautioned him about his drinking. He didn't listen, of course. The medicine made a difference at first. But Antonio was getting worse. He could no longer go to work at the railroad. He stayed home in bed. Aria, though only 12, waited on him and stayed by his bedside night and day. She sang to him and played what she could on the piano to comfort him. He died with Aria holding his hand and singing to him.

Aria was devastated. She had lost her champion, the president of her fan club. Consumed with grief, she turned to her younger sister, Lucia, to fill the void.

They became constant companions. Lucia encouraged Aria to audition for school plays. Aria was in every school play and theatrical production and she sang in her high school's chorus. She thought this was the best way to honor her dear father. She was thrilled when her name was in the *Pittsburgh Gazette* for her performance in a school musical.

Aria was happiest on stage pretending to be someone other than herself. No one was surprised when Aria dramatically announced she was going to be an actress. She had the desire, she was talented, but she lacked her mother's support.

These memories of Aria saddened Rosa. Her daughter had been a difficult child with quite a temper. There were frequent angry outbursts. Aria's temper was usually directed toward her mother—never at her father. Rosa didn't—just couldn't—understand Aria. So much like her father. Rosa appreciated the musical talent but saw no reason to encourage it. Music was fine for at-home entertainment, but Rosa saw no value in voice or piano lessons.

Aria graduated with honors from high school. She was eager to be in the world of music and acting, but Rosa saw a different future for her head-in-the-clouds daughter. Rosa demanded that Aria go to secretarial school to learn shorthand and typing. In 1933, girls were going to business college and working outside of the house. Beautiful and smart Aria would have no trouble finding a clerical position and then a suitable husband. A husband and children would redirect Aria's focus. She would give up these ridiculous notions of the stage and acting.

Surprisingly, Aria agreed to go to the secretarial school. This was her ticket to the stage. She would earn her own money to pay for acting classes. Excelling at everything she did, she was confident she would excel at acting, too.

Upon completing her courses, Aria found a job at Terlizzi's Wurlitzer Piano Store. She was thrilled to be surrounded by music and musicians. And she earned a paycheck. She could have free piano lessons. She could afford acting classes. Aria was on her way to the big stage and a life filled with beautiful clothes. A life away from her mother. Her father would have approved of Aria's plans.

The plan included meeting new people at the annual Wurlitzer Piano Christmas party. It was sponsored by Wurlitzer. Famous musicians, celebrities and company executives were invited. This was an excellent opportunity for Aria to meet people who could further her long-dreamed-of acting career.

Rosa remembered how excited Aria was about the Wurlitzer Store Christmas party. Aria had saved her money to buy some beautiful red taffeta fabric. Her sister, Lucia, was an excellent seamstress. She helped create a gorgeous gown that showed off Aria's petite figure. Lucia surprised her sister with a sparkling faux rhinestone belt buckle with matching buttons. Aria bought a red glass ring to wear with her new dress.

Glass was all she could afford. She thought it was lovely.

Rosa was misty eyed as she remembered how stunningly beautiful her Aria was that night. Rosa suspected there was a man in her life. Aria would never have shared this information with her mother. There was a man, but that wasn't why Aria was excited. She was looking forward to meeting these new and successful people.

The evening was magical and full of promise. Aria met several people who encouraged her and offered to advise her. She was on top of the world. Dancing and singing, she was in her element.

Then the headaches started. Severe blinding headaches. The pain was intense. Aria frequently lashed out at those around her, especially her mother and Lucia. Aria became depressed. She lost her appetite. Food no longer appealed to her. Her behavior changed. She had trouble remembering simple everyday things, such as how to tie her shoes. Lucia would notice that Aria was starting to wear her blouses backwards but wasn't aware she was doing it. Her mind wasn't functioning properly. She was very sick.

Aria had to quit her job because she was so frail. Within a month of leaving Wurlitzer, Aria passed away. The lively, talented and stunning Aria was gone.

Her death certificate listed the cause of death as a sinus infection. The year was 1939. Aria was 24 years old and weighed 58 pounds when she died. The wake was in the family living room. Aria's body was laid out on the sofa. She was buried close to her father's grave. Until the day Rosa passed away, Aria's photo was one of only two photos on Rosa's mantel. The other photo was of her daughter Lucia.

Chapter Nineteen

"We have a possible grandfather for Elaine," I told my husband while we were walking our precious little four-legged fur person. I frequently used our walks to try to process the news that Antonio, formerly known as my grandfather, was not my mother's biological father or my grandfather. "We can't prove it, but I think we are right. I have a couple of possibilities for baby granddaddies." I was trying to add some humor to the confusion in my heart. "I need more information. I just don't know where it will come from. I'm going to keep asking Grandmother Rosa to help me."

"You are convinced the dead can hear you, aren't you?" asked my husband. I know he wanted me to find my family as much as I did. He understood I was feeling lost and rootless.

"I'm positive they hear us."

"How do you talk to them? What do you do?"

"I sit quietly, and simply ask to talk to my grandmother or to Mom or anyone else I want to talk to. Then I just talk to them as if they are in the room or on the phone with me. Just like a regular conversation. I don't expect an answer right away. I just thank them and wait. I have great trust that I will be answered in some form in the coming days."

Later that day, when I was alone, I "talked" to Grandmother Rosa. My plea was honest and sincere. "Grandmother, the jig is up! We know Antonio is not our grandfather. I know he is not Mom's father. I deserve to know the truth. I'm not judging you. I'm hoping nothing bad happened to you that resulted in these pregnancies. I'd like to know my family. I need to know the medical history. Help me with this, please. Thanks."

I knew she heard me. I hoped she would help.

Chapter Twenty

Angelica was looking forward to her visit with Rosa. She had so many questions for her daughter. She was getting over her shock at the stories Rosa had told her about Rosa's marriage to Antonio. Angelica was saddened and angry to hear about the abuse. She couldn't imagine the pain of rejection. Antonio had told Rosa he hated to touch her, he couldn't stand to be in bed with her. Angelica had been very fortunate. Her beloved Emilio rarely drank and was always so kind and compassionate. Theirs was a passionate love story.

Rosa's life wasn't what Angelica had thought it was. She had hoped Rosa was at least content with Antonio. They seemed financially stable. There was a lot of sadness in the beginning with the death of two babies. But then the children started coming. They had six children who lived. Angelica thought the marriage must have been satisfactory or at least tolerable. She never thought Antonio was an abusive and angry drunk. In direct contrast to his contemptible behavior toward Rosa was his acceptance of the children Rosa bore from other men as his own children. He was a difficult and confusing man. The motivation behind his actions remained a mystery to both women.

Angelica was reviewing what she knew about her daughter Rosa's children and their fathers. Antonia, the eldest, was Antonio's biological daughter, while Gianna and Minnie were Gianni's daughters. He was the love of Rosa's life. Armani was Armani Sr.'s son. Beautiful Aria was Antonio's daughter. Why did he seduce Rosa that night? What was that about? Then there was the baby of the family, little Lucia. She knew Rosa was going to tell her that story today.

Mother and daughter had formed a close bond of mutual acceptance and respect. They were encouraging and supportive of each other's spiritual growth in the After Life. Although they both regretted this relationship didn't take place in the Land of the Living, they were grateful they had it now.

Angelica knew Rosa was still concerned about what was going on with Emma in the Land of the Living. Emma and her cohort cousin, Elaine, were uncovering all of Rosa's secrets. She knew Rosa was conflicted over this. Angelica laughed at the number of ways Rosa thought she could thwart Emma's research. Technically, they are not allowed to interfere with people in the Land of the Living, but Rosa found loopholes. Harmless ones. Things like diverting Emma's attention by having her research a different family. That was a little tricky, but Rosa managed it. She bought a little time for herself with that plan. Then there were the times Rosa tried to mess with the internet service. Rosa didn't really understand it, so all she accomplished was to frustrate Emma's husband. Rosa had to let this go. Her job was to help, not sabotage. Her only option was to ignore Emma—and that was tough to do in the After Life. One of the privileges was to hear from the Land of the Living and to help.

Rosa arrived looking frustrated. "It's all unraveling! Emma and that computer machine thingy."

"Rosa, I'm curious how you know so much about what Emma is doing. You know you can't spy on her." Angelica was still Rosa's mother. She still had a duty to teach and hopefully inspire Rosa.

Rosa had found a way around the no spying rule. "It's very simple. I've been talking to my grandchildren. You know several of them have passed on and have joined us here in the After Life. Emma's sister, Marianne, is a wealth of information. That girl loves to talk. Loves to tell stories and talk about other people. She can really dish." Rosa thought she would impress her mother by using current lingo. Her mother was always trying it out on Rosa.

"Dish? You mean serve some food?"

"You are so funny! No, that means to talk about someone, to tell their story."

"Oh, Rosa, you mean gossip?"

"Never mind that, Mom. We have a problem. Emma and Elaine have made a disastrous discovery. They know they are half-first cousins. They now know they have different grandfathers. Emma keeps talking to me. She wants me to help her find her biological grandfather. I just don't know what to do. My whole story is starting to unravel. I'm afraid they will find out the whole truth. We have to do something to stop them."

"You cannot interfere with their actions in the Land of the Living. You cannot stop them from looking into things. You cannot interfere with the use of their computers."

"Not even just a little?" Rosa really wanted to stop Emma.

"What do you have in mind? You haven't been successful so far. I think you might be losing sight of what we are doing here. This is a place and time to face our fears, our problems, our self-doubts. I think you might be hiding from them."

"I'm not worried about facing my past choices. I just don't want everyone in the Land of the Living to know about them."

"Why not?" asked Angelica.

"I am worried what they will think. Emma might be able to guess who her grandfather is, but she won't know why I made the decisions I made. I guess I'm afraid she and her cousins will think less of me. I would like her to quit looking. I was hoping we could think of a diversion. Maybe you could plant some false evidence? Or talk to Elaine or Diana and somehow persuade them to stop Emma. Oh—maybe Emma could have an affair—a love interest to take her mind off her computer machine and research. That would be perfect. Yes, that's it. An affair!"

"Rosa! Oh, my dear daughter. All your hard work on developing the courage to face your past decisions. All of the healing. The progress you've made on your journey to wholeness can be undone by attempting to interfere with Emma's life. Think about your motive. Think about what you are really saying. You are putting what you think people might think about you ahead of your soul's growth. Is that what you really want? And an affair? Really? Rosa, that's terrible."

Rosa was silent. All her lies and misinformation were being exposed. She needed to think this through and not just react. She knew in her heart she needed to do the right thing.

"What is worse, Rosa, impeding or possibly undoing your progress or Emma and Elaine finding out about all your baby daddies?"

"Baby daddies? Where did you get that word? That's awful. Please stop with this trendy talk."

"You said it yourself—our Marianne is a wealth of knowledge."

"Mom, this is serious. I don't know what to do. I don't want to jeopardize the healing I'm experiencing. Keeping all these lies alive and the truth tied up inside of me has become a habit—a part of who I am."

"No, Rosa. They are not a part of who you are. They are just stories you have told. As stories, they can be untold. You can decide to be free of the lies by helping Emma in any way you can."

"I know you are right. I guess I'm not ready yet." Angelica could hear the frustration in her daughter's voice.

"Maybe you could start by telling me the last story you are hiding. Who is Lucia's father?"

"His name was Luca. I met him through my sister Mina about a year and a half after Aria was born. He had moved in next door to her. Her neighbor ran a boarding house and Luca rented a room. He arrived in America and didn't know anyone. Mina felt sorry for him and invited him over for dinner. I happened to stop by while he was still there. He was gracious and entertaining, but underneath the smiles there was something lonely and melancholy about him. I could relate to that. Even though I was married, I was very lonely. I loved being a mother, but I needed more. Luca and I saw each other a couple of times after that. We enjoyed each other's company. We'd flirt a little bit. I'll skip all the details, Mom, but obviously we ended up in bed.

"I had no desire for this to be a long-term relationship. I didn't know how far I could push Antonio with our 'arrangement.' So an ongoing relationship was not a possibility. We saw each other a couple of times a week for several weeks. He was good company. I welcomed the diversion from five children at home and an uninterested and distant husband. I enjoyed the physical connection. We had fun until he told me his wife was on her way to America. Shortly after she arrived, they moved to Maryland. I thought I would never see him again and I was OK with that. Neither of us wanted more. I knew I was pregnant before he moved."

"Did he know he was Lucia's father?"

"Evidently Mina had also befriended his wife. Mina corresponded with her. In one of the letters, she mentioned I was pregnant. Luca figured out that the baby must be his. He knew Antonio and I hadn't been intimate. About six months after Lucia was born, he showed up on Mina's doorstep looking for me. He and his pregnant wife had returned to Pittsburgh. Mina told him where I lived. She didn't know Lucia was his daughter.

"He found me and wanted to see Lucia. I refused. No good could come from it. I had no intention of letting him be involved in her life. Antonio was the only father she was going to know. His own wife was pregnant with their second daughter. I guess he finally understood that I wasn't interested in having him around and he and his wife moved again. I heard that she and her children returned to Italy. Luca made several trips between America and Italy. Mina said she thought he had another family in Maryland. He apparently had an American family and an Italian family. I am so relieved that I did not let him be a part of Lucia's life. I didn't want my unfaithfulness to impact another family."

"Did Lucia know that Antonio was not her biological father?"

"Oh, Mom. There is a terrible story about this." Rosa turned white as she remembered the series of events. Forgiving herself for what happened had proven difficult. Her liaison with Luca came back to haunt Rosa.

"Lucia was always a very bright girl. She excelled in school and was an excellent seamstress. Beyond all of that, she was patient and kind to her sister, Aria. Aria would lash out at Lucia and Lucia would listen until Aria had exhausted herself. Lucia would make her a cup of tea and talk softly to her to calm her down. She was incredible with her. Aria was so domineering. I worried that Lucia would not stand her ground with her. I had very little control over Aria. So much like her father."

Angelica had loved her kind and patient granddaughter, her "Little One," Lucia. "I remember when Little One stayed with me the summer I was so sick. She waited on me like I was royalty. She worked so hard to take care of me. She insisted on doing more than I asked. She was a Godsend. But what does any of this have to do with Lucia and Luca?"

"A couple of months after Lucia graduated from high school, the girls—Lucia and Aria—were preparing to go to the beauty school for an application for Lucia. We couldn't afford college tuition for Lucia. She was pretty and smart—I knew she'd find a husband. Why would she need a college education? So I strongly encouraged her to go to beauty school."

"You mean you insisted—you made her go."

"Yes. While they were upstairs primping, the doorbell rang. Thankfully, I was nearby. I opened the door and there stood Luca, looking older but still Luca with the goofy smile. I was panic stricken. I was afraid the girls would come downstairs and see him. I wouldn't let him in but told him to go to the backyard. The girls were rarely in that little yard, so I thought we'd be safe. He found me thanks to Mina. I don't know what she was thinking. The bottom line is, he was in town for a few days and wanted to see his daughter. I refused, of course. He then asked if her name was Lucia. Mina had inadvertently told him her name. I told him yes, but he was never going to meet her or get to know her. Antonio was dead, so I wasn't afraid of violating our arrangement. I just didn't want Lucia to know. I didn't want her to know what I had done. How would I ever explain it to her?"

Angelica remembered a conversation with her little Lucia. "I understand. I know she accepted Sal as her stepfather and your husband. I also know she had good memories of her father. She would occasionally mention the parties and his accordion playing."

Rosa continued with her story. "Unfortunately, Lucia had come into the backyard to pick some figs. Sal had planted that tree years ago and somehow he got that tree to grow. Picking figs was not an everyday occurrence with Lucia. I had no reason to think she would come out there."

"Did you see her? Did she talk to Luca?"

"No, I didn't see her. I didn't know she overheard us until a few years after that. She didn't talk to Luca. He didn't see her either."

"Then how do you know she knew anything?"

"I'll tell you in a minute. First, let me explain a couple of things. After that day, Lucia was withdrawn and quieter than usual. She was more attached to Aria. Our conversations were few and far apart. I thought she was busy at beauty school. Aria had started having terrible headaches and she was increasingly difficult to be around. Lucia was the only one who could calm her down. Aria would talk back to me and she would get very angry at Lucia. Her anger scared me. Lucia was never scared of her, but she did whatever Aria asked or told her to do. Lucia became quieter and quieter. She seemed sad all the time. They both quit eating. I'm not sure why. Depressed, maybe? They both lost weight rapidly. When Aria died, Lucia was devastated."

"I know how painful a child's death can be." Angelica spoke from experience.

"Lucia, in her grief and misery, confronted me about Luca. I'm not sure why she waited until then. She was too thin and fragile to continue beauty school. Her world was upside down. She looked me right in the eye and told me she knew I was a floozy, and that she was a bastard. She never used words like that, especially directed toward me. Ever. My heart was

142

beating so rapidly—I thought I was going to have a heart attack. I was hoping for one so I wouldn't have to answer her. I thought about reprimanding her for calling me names. But I knew she knew, and I owed her an explanation."

"You told her the truth?"

"I told her an abbreviated version of the truth."

"In other words, you half-lied, half-told the truth?"

"I told her all she needed to know at the time. I told her Antonio and I were going through a very bad time. He was drinking too much and was frequently angry at me. She knew he had a bad temper and drank too much. This wasn't news to her. I wasn't shattering a little girl's dream of her father. I explained to her I wasn't proud of what I did but I was very happy with the result. I loved her very much."

"What did she say? Did that answer satisfy her?" asked Angelica.

"She said she had known the truth for a few years. She told me she had seen me and Luca in the backyard together and overheard our conversation about her. I asked her if that was why she had withdrawn and was so distant. She said she didn't feel like she belonged to the family. She told Aria what she had heard. They both thought they would punish me for my deception. They decided to go on a hunger strike. They thought that would make me look like a bad mother."

"Are you blaming yourself for Aria's death?"

143

"I did blame myself for many years. Finally, a doctor explained to me that her body was shutting down due to the sinus infection. I was not to blame. I didn't cause the infection. I tried to get them to eat. I've finally forgiven myself."

"What about Lucia? Did she forgive you? You two always seemed so close. She was only 13 when I passed over."

"I begged for her forgiveness. She was very sick then. I thought she was going to die, too. Thank God she didn't. I begged for forgiveness so many times. I told her I knew I didn't deserve her forgiveness, but oh how I needed it. When Lucia started feeling better, she found a job. She was stronger, more independent. She was thinking more clearly and becoming her own person. She forgave me and I was thrilled. We were close until the day I died. To my knowledge, she has never told anyone."

"Do you think she told her brother? They were so close."

"I don't know. He never said anything to me about Luca. I know she didn't tell Emma."

"How would you know that?" Angelica was curious.

"Emma keeps talking to me from the Land of the Living. She keeps telling me I have some explaining to do. She blames me for her mother's weight loss and illness. I don't know how to fix that from here while she is still in the Land of the Living. I promise to tell her as soon as I can after she arrives here. She is persistent with her questions. She is egged on by her cousin, our Elaine."

"I'm sure she'll have lots of questions when she sees us. I have one more question for you, if you don't mind. Was there anyone after Luca?"

"No. I was done with men and relationships. I focused all my attention on my children. I shoved my loneliness way down inside of me. Antonia married when Lucia was only six months old. I had plenty to do to avoid thinking about having any connection with another man."

"Until Antonio died...."

"I guess I should have expected his death. All that drinking was killing him. His doctor warned him, but Antonio wouldn't listen. I was free of his abuse and released from our unusual living situation, but I needed money. When Aunt Louisa suggested I marry Sal, I agreed. He was a hard worker, he was frugal, he had a savings account. He could support me and the three children who were still living at home. I wanted Armani to go to college and Sal had the money for that. We knew each other in Italy. You remember that, don't you?"

"Of course, he is your first cousin!"

"No, my first cousin once removed. I did fudge on that detail when I told the children I was remarrying. They think he is a distant cousin. I had to say something because we had the same last name."

"Emma will find that out, too, you know!"

"I know, but I'm not worried. Mom, I do have a question for you. Do you know what became of the man your parents wanted you to marry in Italy? Wasn't his name Giovanni? Was he brokenhearted over your refusal to marry him?"

Angelica laughed. "No, he wasn't brokenhearted. He was in love with a neighbor who was eight years older than he. His parents didn't like the match because they thought she wasn't a good housekeeper and was too old. She wouldn't be able to have many children. He married her against their wishes. They emigrated to America and lived in New York. He was very successful."

"Oh, tell me! Did he start a pizza business that grew into a large national chain?"

"No, Rosa, he was an architect. His first wife had four children. They were well off. They lived in a large house with maids and a kitchen staff. His wife died and he remarried. This time he married a much, much younger woman. They had six more children. He was around ninety-four when he died. There was newspaper coverage of his funeral. He was also on the cover of an architectural magazine. He was very successful and extremely wealthy."

"That could have been your life, Mom."

"No, I only wanted Emilio."

Chapter Twenty-one

Ten days had passed since I told my grandmother that the jig was up and I knew Antonio was not my grandfather. I asked for her help. I was still shocked. I still couldn't wrap my brain around the loss of part of my family. My family tree was very lopsided. I had run out of ideas how to find my grandfather's family—my family.

I was online looking at my tree when I noticed I had a message. There was a very short email from someone I hadn't contacted. The message was, "Hi. I'm Claire in Italy. We are related." She didn't ask any questions or ask for a response. I checked our DNA results and we did share some cMs. When I looked at her tree, I didn't see any familiar surnames. I always respond to people who reach out to me regarding ancestry research, so I responded to Claire with some family names. Her response was waiting for me the next day. She didn't recognize any of my family's names either. Truthfully, I was intrigued by the timing of her correspondence and my request to my grandmother for some help. I decided to be more forthcoming with Claire.

I told her that I had recently discovered that my grandfather wasn't my grandfather. My grandmother had a liaison that resulted in the birth of my mother. I didn't know who my grandfather was.

Her response was, "We're confused, too. We have always thought my great-grandfather had a second family in America. He made several trips back and forth from Italy to America."

I was doubtful but hopeful. There was never any hint of another "father" in my mom's life. So I was skeptical. I looked at Claire's tree again, then I started my own research into her great-grandfather, Luca Esposito.

He was in the Pittsburgh area around the time my mother would have been conceived. He lived in a boarding house. His wife immigrated after he did. They moved to Maryland after being in Pittsburgh for several months. They were in Maryland for a couple of years. Then he returned to Pittsburgh for a few months. Luca, his wife and two children returned to Italy. His wife and children remained in Italy.

I then found four more round trips from Italy to the States. I also discovered that he worked in Maryland, dying in 1979 when he was in his 90's. But none of this proved he was my grandfather. I found his picture on a legal document and didn't see any family resemblance.

Claire offered to email pictures of his Italian family. I opened the email with the photos wondering if they would be helpful. Would there be any family resemblance? Included in the family photos were several photos of Luca's daughter, Alicia. She would be Mom's half-sister. The photos ranged from childhood to adulthood. I stared and stared at them. Staring back at me was a woman who looked like my sister, Marianne. Actually, she could have been my sister the resemblance was so strong. My heart stopped. Was this my new family?

I thought I was seeing what I wanted to see. I showed the screen to my husband to ask him if Alicia looked familiar. His immediate response was, "She looks like Marianne."

I emailed the pictures to Elaine with the same question. Her response, "She looks like Marianne."

I was incredulous. Was Luca my mother's father? Was Alicia my mother's half-sister? I hoped so. My new cousin, Claire, is a delightful, cheerful soul. We have a lot in common in our interests and approach to life. We are both looking for answers. I think we may have found some.

Claire and I stay in touch via email. For my birthday, she baked a cake for me. She lives near Rome, Italy, and I live in West Virginia. She couldn't send the cake to me, but she wanted to honor my special day. She ate the cake for me! I was so touched by her thoughtfulness. I'm grateful she is part of my family.

I had another email from Claire today. She might travel to New York this year. We'll do everything we can to meet her in person. I'm eager to meet her.

I already knew our loved ones who have passed over are around us. I knew they could hear us. I've had several experiences in my life to confirm this. I knew Grandmother Rosa could hear me. However, I didn't know if she would help me. I don't think she is compelled to help. I like to think she wants to guide us and to help us find our roots and one another.

"Thanks, Grandmother Rosa. I appreciate the help," I whispered, "and you still have some explaining to do."

Chapter Twenty-two

"Rosa, you look beautiful! So happy. You seem lighter and brighter." Angelica was pleased to see her daughter. The last time they visited, Rosa was stressing about Emma's newest research. Emma knew Antonio was not her grandfather. She asked Rosa for help in finding her biological grandfather. Rosa was unsure she wanted to help her granddaughter.

"I feel much better. I did some soul searching. I realized I was hurting the people I love. I was hurting myself, too. I shoved my self-respect aside and wanted to take what seemed like the easy way out. I wanted to continue to hide my life, my truth."

"What did you decide to do?"

"I did some nudging. Emma now knows who her grandfather is. She has connected with her new family and she is so happy with this discovery. I am overjoyed with her response. She didn't judge me. She thanked me. She knows there must be a good reason for my relationship with Luca. I am so relieved."

Angelica was filled with admiration for her daughter and told her so. Their souls were finally at peace.

"I have a couple of questions," Rosa said. She thoroughly enjoyed their conversations. They were comfortable with each other, and conversation could flow easily. "Do you remember being sick before you died? Do you remember when you passed over from the Land of the Living to here?"

"I do. I know I was sick for about 18 months. What I remember is not the illness, the doctors or the medicine. I remember my family and friends taking care of me. There were neighbors I didn't know very well who brought food to us. Some of the food didn't appeal to me because I was sick. But the food was still appreciated. My family needed to eat. People were so thoughtful. I felt loved. The flowers your children brought me were beautiful, they lifted my spirits. I knew people were praying for me. I could feel a sense of divine peace growing inside my soul. I knew this was a gift from God sent to me in answer to their prayers. I was so grateful for their concern about my comfort. "

"We thought you were in pain."

"I was in pain, but the pain was made bearable by the love I felt from all of you. I was surrounded by people who loved me. I could feel the love filling every cell in my body. What a wonderful sensation. I was grateful for everyone there. Their strength gave me strength."

"We didn't know if you knew we were there."

"Of course I knew! Your love transcended the fact that my body was coming to an end. Love lives forever. I was aware of everyone in the room. I was also aware of the people you couldn't see. My parents visited numerous times while I was sick."

"I thought they were furious with you about Dad."

"They forgave me right before they passed away. They were able to visit me because I was going to join them in the After Life. We knew the time was near. They were sent to help me prepare for my next journey. Those visits were wonderful. My grandparents were also around me. They escorted me to the After Life. I was greeted by so many people who loved me and whom I loved. There was a glorious reunion. So many hugs and kisses. And the laughter. We had such fun!"

"Was Dad there?"

"I could sense Emilio, but I didn't see him. My husband was there, of course. Your dear sister Bella and brother Francesco were there, too. Do you remember your passing?"

Rosa started to laugh. "Yes! I do. Do you remember Mozzi's Bakery on Green Avenue?"

"What delicious cakes and those cannoli. Oh, I remember!"

"I walked by there every time I went to the market or on my way to Mass. I was going to Mass daily then. So, I passed that delicious smelling bakery every day. Do you know that I never bought a treat for myself? I purchased a cake for Lucia's wedding and a cake for one of Armani's birthdays, but never anything for myself. The night before my passing over to the After Life, I decided I was going to buy a piece of chocolate cake. I didn't want to bake a whole one for myself. I was finally going to treat myself after Mass. The next morning I put money in my handbag—I usually didn't carry money with me. I was approaching the bakery, the smell of bread baking filled the street. I was eager to see what was in the window. There was always some delectable, layered cake on display. That particular day there was a seven-layer chocolate cake—'Seventh Heaven-Death by Chocolate'! I remember thinking I would like to jump into the middle of that cake and eat my way out.

"Next thing I knew, I was filled with a wonderful sensation, a sensation of joy and love. Then I saw my children who had passed over before me, Gianna, Minnie and Aria. The babies were there, too. I wasn't sure what was happening, but I was not frightened. There was so much joy and love—love that exceeded the love I experienced in the Land of the Living. Gianna explained I had passed over and they escorted me to the After Life."

"I remember the party we had to celebrate your arrival. Did you see your father?"

"I did see him briefly. He told me he loved me, but he couldn't stay. I somehow understood what he was telling me. We were thrilled to see one another even if it was only for a few minutes."

"I didn't see Antonio at the welcome party. Did you see him or the other baby daddies?" Angelica was laughing. She knew Rosa didn't like her to use that expression.

"What. Ev. Er. Mo. Ther," responded Rosa with a newfound gaiety in using slang to impress her mother.

"Oh, look at you! Where did you learn that?"

"Marianne! You aren't the only one who talks to her."

"You didn't answer my question—did you see Antonio or anyone else?"

"Antonio stood with Aria for a while. I saw him, but we didn't speak. There was no animosity—just no need to speak at that time. And no, none of the 'others' were there. I know we have more work to do before we see each other."

Rosa knew the day would come when she would see the men in her life. She welcomed the opportunity to talk to each one of them. There was such unfinished business with Antonio. She really wanted an explanation about their marriage and their "arrangement." She especially wanted to see her beloved Gianni. Soon, she hoped. Soon.

"One more question, Mom. Have you seen Dad? I haven't seen him since he greeted me when I passed over. I haven't talked to Gianni either. I know this isn't a woman-only After Life. There are plenty of men here—just not our men."

"When they have come to terms with their choices, their fears and misgivings, we will see them. They will be free to visit with anyone they choose. I do hope it is soon. I'd love to see Emilio."

"On a lighter note, I'd still love to jump into the Seventh Heaven-Death by Chocolate cake." Both women laughed until they had tears in their eyes.

The journey was long and arduous—they had finally arrived at a place of understanding, kindness, compassion, love and laughter. The After Life was good.

Chapter Twenty-three

Covid restrictions were finally lifted. We could go to a restaurant. To celebrate the occasion, my good friend JB and I went shopping and to lunch. JB and I share a love of fabric and shopping for fabric. Our favorite store is about a two-hour drive from our homes. The drive gives us plenty of time to get caught up on recent events and to tell stories.

"Were you close to your mother?" JB didn't know my mother. We had met a few years after our mothers had passed over. We were sharing mother stories. It was my turn.

"My mom was difficult to get to know." What an understatement. I didn't want to bombard JB with all the details of a very troubled relationship. She already knew the twisted tale of "my grandfather isn't my grandfather/Mom's dad isn't her biological dad."

"She was always guarded about her family. Sometimes she would share some information, other times she would become irritated if I asked a question. I wonder now if she knew about her biological father."

"Do you think she knew? Did she say something to make you think she knew?" JB asked.

"No. I only know bits and pieces of my mom's history. I'm still trying to make sense of what I know and what I have researched."

We had reached our destination and fabric shopping consumed us. The question "Do you think she knew?" haunted me. I needed to think about this.

Later that evening, I had time to think. I decided to write down what I knew about Mom that might help me answer the question: did she know?

The first big event in her life that was life-changing was the death of Antonio, the man she knew as her father. He died December 19, 1925. Mom was 10. Her closest sister, Aria, was devoted to their father. Aria was devastated and turned to Mom for comfort. That is a heavy burden for a 10-year-old.

Also in 1925, Mom's sister, Minnie, who was married and had a two-year-old son, became ill. She was diagnosed with tuberculosis. Minnie returned to her mother's house so Rosa could take care of her, but she died shortly after her arrival. She was only 21 years old.

So, Mom had lost her father and her sister within months of each other. She never talked to me about what she experienced or how she felt. I tried, but she'd give only basic facts. She did mention when she was in school, she was placed in a special room with lots of windows and sunshine. She was given extra graham crackers to eat and milk to drink. She said it was because she was sickly. I think the sadness at home was affecting Mom's health. Again, she wouldn't elaborate even though I asked questions, hoping for more details. She was so guarded. I thought maybe the memories were too painful and talking about them brought up all the grief again. I don't know.

I know the relationship between Mom and her sister, Aria, was tough on Mom. They were very close, but Aria had a terrible temper. Mom said it was usually directed toward her mother. Aria was extremely dramatic and wanted to be an actress. She also loved beautiful clothes. For some reason Mom was expected to wash and curl Aria's hair.

This was a one-sided arrangement—Aria did not reciprocate. Mom told me her mother and Aria would insist that she curl her sister's hair. Aria wore her jet-black hair in what we called "long curls." Mom would part Aria's long hair into one-inch sections. She would wrap each section around a long thin rag. When the rags were dry, Mom would untie them. This produced a very long ringlet, a "long curl." I know this technique well. Mom did the same thing to my hair. I remember the rags could be tied too tight and it hurt. I wasn't overly thrilled with the "long curls." I thought they were too young for me and old fashioned. This finally stopped when I was 12. I don't remember Mom using these rag curls on my sister. However, many years later, I was expected to wash and curl my sister's hair. We used "rollers" in the 1960s. I didn't enjoy it and it wasn't reciprocated either. Was history repeating itself?

Mom graduated from high school with the highest honors. Loving to learn, she dreamed of going to college. Her mother didn't think Mom needed to go to college. Grandmother had said they couldn't afford it. She could send her only son to college, but not her highly intelligent daughter. If I know nothing else about my mother, I do know this—she wanted to go to college more than anything. Her dreams were shattered by her mother's unwillingness to help her. Her mother insisted upon beauty school, which was affordable. And didn't Lucia already have experience in doing hair? All those years of washing and curling Aria's hair had been her prep for beauty school. Mom was obedient and went to beauty school.

This is when the health of both Mom and Aria began to decline. Something happened. Something more than the unrelentless disappointment of not going to college. But what happened? What pushed Mom and Aria over the edge?

The only thing Mom would say about this time in her life was, "Everywhere I turned, I hit a wall." One of those walls was being told she was too frail to complete beauty school. Mom had lost so much weight. She walked miles to beauty school because she didn't have bus fare. The owners of the school told her she wasn't healthy enough to finish school and certainly not healthy enough to stand all day doing hair.

She and Aria were both home due to their loss of weight and resulting poor health. Aria could no longer work at her Wurlitzer job. Mom said Aria loved working there.

I remember the day I asked Mom about Aria's death. All she said was Aria had terrible headaches. Aria's temper was worse because she was sick. Aria wore her blouses backwards but didn't know she was doing that. Then she died. No details.

"I was in the hospital when she died. I had a lump removed from my leg. My aunt came into the hospital room and said, 'Your sister has died. Get dressed. You are going home.'" Mom's voice was flat as she repeated what her aunt said. I wonder, is this how Mom heard her aunt's voice? Void of compassion or sympathy?

That was all Mom said. I asked how old Aria was when she died. Mom's response? "I was 22. She was 2 ½ years older. You figure it out." Seriously, that was her answer. Wow. I guess that was grief talking. Aria had been gone for 60 years when we had that conversation.

A couple of years after that, I was going through some of my old high school stuff in Mom's basement. I looked in a trunk and found a beautiful, bright pinkish handmade dress. I guessed it was a size 2 or smaller. It had a marvelous fake rhinestone belt buckle and buttons. I loved it. I ran upstairs to ask Mom about it. Her face turned beet red. She quietly said, "That was Aria's." I apologized for showing it to her and bringing up painful memories. "The tears have all been cried," was her response. "Aria wore that to the Terlizzi's Wurlitzer Piano Christmas party." I'll never forget the look on her face. I still have the red dress that had faded to a shade of pink. I've taken the belt buckle off, put it on a chain and have worn it as a necklace. I suffered from horrible, debilitating headaches when I was younger. I can only imagine a little of what my beautiful Aunt Aria suffered. I would like to have known her.

My heart aches for my mom and Aria. I often wonder what my grandmother was thinking when Aria and Mom stopped eating. Did she talk to them? Did their older sisters try to help? When did they become aware that Aria was ill, and that her illness was causing her mood swings and angry outbursts? Did she have any medical attention? Grandmother Rosa, you have some explaining to do. You were their mother. They lived at home with you. Where were you? Obviously, I blame her for their health issues.

After Aria's death, Mom's health declined rapidly, she lost more weight. Thankfully, her brother's best friend since childhood was now a doctor. Dr. Levi Cohen convinced a home for unwed mothers and convalescents into admitting Mom. Sixty some years later, Elaine found a letter from her dad to her mother. Uncle Armani mentioned that the doctors made a bet they could get Mom to gain weight. They bet she could go from 68 pounds to 100 pounds in a year.

Mom had another champion in her corner. The owner of the home, Mrs. Schmidt, said what Mom needed was some "company" and some "attention." I think this is heart wrenching. My tears have not all been

164

cried. This is difficult to write about. Mom's heart was broken by her sister's death. Who was there to comfort her? Why was Mom so neglected at home? I know the loneliness of being in a house with other people and having a clear sense that you don't belong there—there isn't room for you. Was this my mom's experience? Why?

A complete stranger, my hero, Mrs. Schmidt, reached out to my mother and saved her life. Mrs. Schmidt was determined Mom was going to not just survive but to thrive. She allowed Mom to eat dinner with her. If Mrs. Schmidt had an errand to run, she took Mom with her when possible. She gave her attention and companionship.

The doctors provided the medical attention Mom needed. Mom didn't talk about the medical aspect of her stay at the home, but she spoke fondly of Mrs. Schmidt. I have the newspaper clipping of her obituary. Mom saved it for years. I will continue to save it.

I keep thinking something must have happened to make Mom and Aunt Aria quit eating. Because their weight loss is well known in the family, I mentioned to Mom that a cousin had said something about how thin she and Aunt Aria were. I said people thought they intentionally didn't eat. Mom, true to her no-details-responses said, "We did some foolish things. We made some stupid choices." The End. No more discussion. That was all I was going to get. If I pushed for more information, she would become angry and tell me she had work to do. I hated making my mom angry at me, so I stopped asking questions.

I know Mom thrived at the home. After a year as a convalescent, and now weighing 100 pounds, she was employed there for a couple of years. I'm not sure why she left but she returned to her mother's house and worked at a hospital. According to Mom, Uncle Armani came over to see her and she was crying. She was unhappy in that house, again. This was 1942. Uncle Armani told Mom about Women Ordinance Workers. They were part of the U.S. Army and they needed women. These were good paying jobs with benefits and some travel. This was her ticket out of the house and the indwelling sadness and grief. Mom applied and was accepted.

Joining the Women Ordinance Workers was a huge turning point in my mother's life. She was transferred to Wheeling, West Virginia. Mom was on her way to a healthier and happier life and on her way to my dad.

So, that is what I knew about Mom's early life. Sickly child, two deaths close together when she was 10, stepfather when she was 11, high school graduation with highest honors, no money for the much dreamed of college education, forced to go to beauty school, forced out of beauty school because of poor health, unexplained weight loss and the devastating death of her best friend and sister, Aria.

Between beauty school and Aria's death something happened. Something traumatic. What if Mom was in the home for unwed mothers because she was pregnant and not because she was sick? I researched the home online, finding that it is no longer a home for unwed mothers but an addiction center. I called anyway and was directed to an archivist. A very kind man said he would look up Mom's records and call me. He returned my call the next day, saying he had her records. I told him part of Mom's story and I hoped she wasn't there because she was pregnant. He said he couldn't divulge any information over the phone. Then he thoughtfully added, "You don't need to lose any sleep over a pregnancy." God bless this man. I was so relieved. My theory was wrong.

I received her records. Mom had a few different diagnoses—some female problems, an infection and anemia. It was noted she had had "no menstrual periods for seven years" and "no left ovary," and that "a small mass could be the right ovary." Oh, Mom, what did you do to yourself? And why?

"I have a new theory about my mom." I think my husband may have groaned but he covered it well. "I think she may have found out that Antonio wasn't her biological father. I think she found out sometime around the time she went to beauty school. You've seen her high school picture. She looks great! It is one of my favorite pictures of her. I'm not sure how much time elapsed from high school to beauty school. I know she was disappointed about not going to college. I just know something more must have happened to her."

"Wasn't your aunt sick, too?"

"Yes. I'm sure that had an impact on Mom—I know it did. But not enough for Mom to go downhill like that. Something happened. I really think she found out about a sexual relationship between her mom and some man. And she was the result of this affair. She loved her mom. This would have been traumatic—life changing even."

"You said she loved her mother. How does that work with your theory? Wouldn't she have been angry with her mother for sleeping with another man?"

"Maybe they talked it through? Mom forgave her? I'd like to think Grandmother had her reasons for making the choices she made."

We walked in silence. Our little baby dog was patrolling her territory and scent marking. The walk was taking a long time. "Do you remember when we were visiting with your cousin, River? He asked an interesting question. He asked me if I had forgiven my grandmother for having an affair. I'm glad he asked. I'm not angry at her nor do I think she did anything I need to forgive her for. I keep clinging to the idea that she must have had a good reason to have at least three different fathers for her children."

"What do you think that reason was?" asked my husband.

"That, I don't know. Still working on it. I'm still asking her. She does have some explaining to do."

Chapter Twenty-four

Emilio was aware his Angelica had joined him in the After Life. He was there when she arrived escorted by her loving grandparents. She looked wonderful. He was allowed to be there, and she was allowed to feel his presence, but she couldn't see him. Emilio understood the goal of the After Life and the rules that supported this goal.

The goal was the same for everyone. The path might differ, the timing might differ, even your attitude might differ. But the goal was the same: healing the soul, healing the pain the soul carried over from the Land of the Living. Pain caused by fear. Fear caused people to say thoughtless, hurtful things. Fear caused people to do terrible things to one another. Uncovering this fear was each person's individual journey.

Everyone who ever lived and passed over was in the After Life. Everyone was given an opportunity to self-reflect and to heal. Each healing journey was different. Facing your truth was essential. Facing your truth can be interpreted as facing who you were in the Land of the Living.

The After Life is a gift. The more you are willing to heal, the more you heal. The more you tell yourself the truth about your life, the further you progress on your journey. If you choose to hang on to all your fears, you can. You will not progress, and you cannot see your loved ones.

This is what Emilio had chosen to do. He held his old fears in his heart and soul as if he had used some type of super adhesive. He wasn't going to examine his life, his decisions, his choices or his actions. Nothing. Just sit there and do nothing. Time is different in the After Life but since Emilio had passed over, he had made no progress. That was about to change.

One of Emilio's great-grandchildren, whom he shared with his beautiful Angelica Caserta, had just passed over. He was allowed to peek into her arrival and the celebration party. He could not attend. As usual when this happened, Emilio first looked for Angelica. Sometimes he would see her, sometimes he just sensed her. He was content with that until today.

There she was. She looked different. Angelica was radiant. Such a serene peacefulness on her face. She was laughing and talking, and she seemed so happy. He intuitively knew why she looked different and so radiant. He had seen this look on other people.

She had faced her truth and examined their life together. She had told their children the truth. Emilio missed her and his heart ached. He wanted to talk to her so much it hurt.

He knew what he needed to do to talk to her. He must face his actions from his life in the Land of the Living. Emilio was inspired by her courage. He drank it in. He absorbed her radiance. He was finally ready. Where to begin?

"I'll start with the beginning," he said to himself.

Emilio was from a small family in southern Italy. He had one sister. They had been very close growing up. They had numerous aunts and uncles who lived close to one another and who formed a tight knit group. Emilio was the only grandson. He was surrounded by females, and he loved it. His grandparents doted on their only male heir, their precious Emilio. He admitted to himself, he was spoiled by his entire family. Whatever Emilio wanted Emilio got. This included the attention of female admirers.

Emilio was handsome with his dark hair and his brown eyes. He knew his eyes were his best feature. He used them to get what he wanted. There were plenty of girls he wanted. The list was too long for Emilio to remember all of them. Emilio understood women and how to talk to them. He had learned from his mom, sister and so many female cousins. He remembered always having a girlfriend or two or three.

He also loved his God and wanted to serve Him. Emilio thought he could best serve God as a priest. He was well aware of the sacrifices involved. He understood the vows of poverty, chastity and obedience that he would have to make. He would own nothing. He would be required to lead a chaste life, without sex, no girlfriends, no wives. He would go where he was sent. Emilio liked this new exclusive community of chosen men to follow and serve God. He was set apart from others. He was special—or so he thought.

Now, in the After Life, reviewing his decision, he realizes how shortsighted he had been. He did indeed like to help people. He was a people person with a kind and gentle manner. He had an ability, a talent actually, of helping people. He was a good listener, people would pour their pained souls out to him. He would talk with them and pray with them.

He also realized he loved women and a domestic life. He loved the idea of sharing his life with a woman and having children. His own mother had told him on numerous occasions that she had raised him to love and be loved. His relationships with women had been encouraged by his family. His decision to enter the priesthood was a shock to them. Emilio was persuasive and used to getting his way. This was no exception. What Emilio wanted Emilio got. Therefore, Emilio made his vows. He was Father Emilio.

After a while, though, the novelty of his supposed specialness of being a priest wore off. He missed female companionship and the tender touch of a woman. There were still plenty of women around. What would be wrong with a harmless flirtation? He was an itinerant priest, which meant he traveled from community to community celebrating Mass and the sacraments. He filled in for other priests when the need arose. He could flirt a little, leave town, flirt a little in another town and leave. Perfect set up.

Emilio was content with this until he met the incredibly beautiful and alluring Philomena. He followed his now established pattern of flirting. The eye contact that lingered just a little longer than a friendly glance. The type of contact that touches female fantasies. He was well accomplished at this, and he knew it. The embrace that lasted a few seconds longer. The well-practiced laughter and engaging conversation. This felt good to Emilio. He didn't think his conduct violated his vows.

Philomena didn't see it that way. She knew what was behind those long looks and embraces. She knew there was a deeper desire. She felt it and she knew he did, too.

Emilio closed his eyes. He wanted to escape from his past, not examine it. This facing your truth or, in his case, his deception was tough. If he wanted to heal this pain, he needed to face what he had done.

He meant no ill will to anyone. He missed women. Philomena was more than willing. He succumbed to their physical desires aided by a little too much wine. He had a sexual encounter with her. Wine and a natural desire, that is how he rationalized his actions. He was remorseful and disappointed in himself. But wait! Maybe he and Philomena had something special. He would see her again. Maybe he would know if this was more than lust. He had sex with her again just to prove to himself this wasn't a one-night stand, but that he cared about her. "That was crazy thinking. That makes no sense," Emilio said to himself. That was just an excuse to be in her bed again. He knew that then but wouldn't admit it to himself. Now he was facing the lie he had told himself and told Philomena.

If this had been his only lapse, Emilio would have forgiven himself years ago while still in the Land of the Living. After those two encounters with Philomena, he made a promise to himself, no more flirting. He kept this promise until he was on a weeklong vacation to a small, out of the way town. He was going there just to relax and recharge. The last year had been long and lonely. He wanted time to think. A few days off was granted. He stayed with the local priest, Father Umberto.

Father Umberto was a cheerful, happy man. He was very content with his calling to be a priest. He enjoyed working with the families in their small town. He told Emilio about a family, the Casertas, who were having trouble convincing their daughter to marry. She was 22 and should already be married but her head was filled with silly notions. Her parents told him she wanted to feel a connection with her husband. She wanted to be in love. She was refusing an arranged marriage. Her grandparents were on her side. The Casertas needed to be practical. They needed their daughters to marry into financial stability. They found the perfect man for one of them. Her desire for "connectedness" was not a factor in their decision. Their daughter was a good Catholic girl. They knew she would listen to Father Umberto. They enlisted his help. He would talk to her this Sunday after Mass.

Emilio liked this small town. No one knew him there. He was free to be himself. He could walk, go to the local shops and not be recognized. He was happy.

Happier than he had been in this long flirtless year. When Sunday arrived, Father Umberto pointed out the Caserta family and their daughter. Emilio said he would talk to the daughter and encourage her to listen to her parents. Perfect plan, they thought.

"You must be Angelica!" Emilio looked into the very beautiful, unsuspecting face of Angelica Caserta. He knew how to draw her in, to engage her in a conversation. Emilio put forth his best effort. He was charming. He noticed the look in her eyes. He had seen that look before. It said, "He is a priest, don't flirt, be polite and walk away!" He knew how to deal with that. And deal he did. He poured on the charm and the laughter and the long looks into her eyes. This was easy for him to do. He was an expert in getting people to talk. And she was beautiful. Just as he planned, she was laughing and talking with him. The "be polite and walk away" look was gone. Success was his.

"Why did I do that to her?" he asked himself. "She didn't deserve that." Finally, Emilio was feeling the grace of the After Life. The grace to face your life, own your actions and forgive yourself. Forgiveness was yet to come. Emilio had more, lots more thinking to do. The more he thought about his actions that day the more Emilio wept. He had deceived her.

He remembered he saw Angelica again a few days later. She was fun. This time, Emilio had no hidden agenda. He allowed himself to be himself. That was easy to do around her. Conversation flowed effortlessly. They talked about everything. He could tell her anything, but he did not tell her about Philomena. He saw Angelica every day. They had a secret meeting place. He loved his time with her. He was Emilio, not Father Emilio. That feeling was intoxicating, addicting, he wanted more.

Leaving was difficult. He told her he would write. Looking back, he wasn't sure if that was sincere about writing. What would be the purpose? This had been fun, but he didn't want to go down that road again. The escapade with Philomena had taught him that lesson.

Emilio returned to his routine of traveling, celebrating Mass, talking to parishioners, helping those in need. Something was missing. He had no one to talk to—no one who cared about what was going on with him. He missed Angelica. He decided to write to her. The effects of a couple of extra glasses of wine mixed with his loneliness helped him write a romantic note. True or not, it was romantic. He told her he would be a fool not to be in love with her. This was true but he shouldn't have said it. He knew that now. This just opened the door for all things disastrous.

Angelica took his words seriously. Their correspondence became more passionate. Thoughts of Angelica filled his heart. He daydreamed about her. He longed for her at night. Their relationship had been chaste, but his longings were not. Emilio was hooked. What started out as a game with him had backfired. He was in love.

What to do with this love was something Emilio should have thought and prayed about. Instead, he just reacted. He had to see Angelica again.

Plans were made. The reunion with Angelica was magical. He was Emilio again. He thought he was free to love her when he was around her. They created their own world. He wanted to touch her, to hold her, to kiss her, but she refused his advances. Emilio was filled with passionate desire. But duty called and again he had to leave.

More letters followed. Letters filled with love, support, desire. He used his signature line, "I want to hold you so close not even moonlight can come between us." He liked that line because it was always successful. Emilio always got what Emilio wanted. He wanted Angelica.

Even in the After Life, Emilio was embarrassed thinking about their first time together. He finally convinced Angelica of his love for her. He already knew she loved him. His dreams about being with her were finally coming true. But his body wouldn't respond. Was God protecting her? Probably.

They should have left things there, but they didn't. Their desires were fulfilled. They were happy together. They brought out the best in each other. They were in love. When they were together, the priesthood didn't exist.

However, when they were apart, there was pain and guilt. Emilio abruptly stopped his review of his life. He

177

realized the pain and the guilt were not because he had not lived up to his vows, but because he never had any intention of leaving the priesthood for Angelica or having any committed relationship with her. His heart stopped for a moment with this realization. They always said they felt guilty because they had offended God by betraying his vows. This wasn't the truth for Emilio. He had to face that now.

He liked the idea of being a priest, but his vows were just words to him. He didn't mind the poverty vow. His parents and grandparents gave him money. Obedience was easy. He loved being an itinerant priest. He was free of the restrictions of a parish and nosey parishioners. Chastity? He loved to love and be loved. He wasn't willing to give that up.

Could he ever forgive himself so he could start to heal? He knew he would have to tell Angelica the truth. That was the process in the After Life. Tell yourself the truth, tell others the truth. Forgive yourself and forgive others. Emilio had a long road ahead of him.

Finally admitting this to himself gave him courage to continue. He was beginning to feel a little lighter, think a little more clearly. The burden of a life built on lies was being slowly lifted.

He moved forward, remembering the early days with Angelica and facing his buried lies. He knew he loved Angelica. She was easy to love. She put her life on hold to accommodate his needs. She was always there for him. He took advantage of her love and devotion. He had everything he wanted. He enjoyed his role of being a priest and he had the warmth of a beautiful woman who loved him. He traveled. He didn't have roots. Life was good for Emilio in the Land of the Living. His life was a lie, but Emilio didn't see it that way. Lies were easy to bury in the Land of the Living.

Emilio caught his breath as he remembered the awful day Angelica told him she was pregnant. He was horrified. His world came crashing down. This was supposed to be a fun relationship that served his selfish needs. He didn't need a pregnant woman. He didn't want a baby. He didn't want or need the responsibility. There was no way he was going to go talk to her parents about this dilemma. He expected they would be angry and demand she never see him again. He could live with that. Might be hard at first, but he'd get over it.

Her parents surprised him, they kicked her out of the house and disowned her. She was now his responsibility. This was his worst-case scenario. Thankfully, her grandparents came to the rescue. They provided financial help. Angelica and Emilio moved in together in a small house outside of town.

Emilio smiled with tears of joy in his eyes as he remembered the day his first daughter was born. She was beautiful, so tiny, so perfect. They named her Rosa. That was his grandmother's name. Emilio was in love again! He was smitten by his daughter. His life was fuller than ever. He had everything he could ever want. Life was good, for a while.

But his other life as a priest had to be addressed. He knew Angelica hoped he would decide to leave the priesthood and marry her. They had talked about it. She made it very clear he had to decide between the priesthood or not the priesthood. The decision was not between being a priest or being with her. Angelica did not want to be the reason he left the priesthood. She needed him to have the strength to decide for himself. No ultimatums from her.

He had to leave Angelica to fulfill his priestly duties. He couldn't stay with her any longer. He was still a priest and had responsibilities.

Angelica started a terrible fight with him. No, wait. That wasn't true. That was just the story he was accustomed to telling. He needed to tell the truth now. He started a fight because he felt so guilty at leaving Angelica and Rosa. He also had made the decision to leave her permanently. He could not live there with her anymore. He didn't want the commitment and responsibilities. He started the fight so he could be justified in leaving and not returning. He knew Angelica was devastated. But she'd get over it. She had Rosa, who needed her attention.

Emilio reflected on those days without Angelica and Rosa. The freedom felt so good. The elevated position of being a priest felt good. He enjoyed the travel. He had friends in the small towns he was assigned to. His responsibilities were few.

He was celebrating Mass one Sunday when he noticed a man and a woman with their infant daughter. He could feel his heart breaking, his soul dying. He missed Angelica and their Rosa. He wanted to go home to them.

This way of life continued for years. He wasn't sure if Angelica knew how many times he planned to leave and never return. But every time he returned. Their passion created more children. He loved having infants, toddlers, children. He loved everything about their innocence, laughter and even their dependence on him. He and Angelica had an arrangement. He would leave to fulfill his duties as an itinerant priest, then he would return to work on the farm. Between the financial support of her grandparents, his parents and their farm, they had what they needed to live.

Emilio would like to leave the story there. They had an arrangement, it worked. He didn't want to think about what happened next.

He sat in silence, clearing his thoughts and soaking in the new sense of lightness. He wasn't sure of what healing felt like. He guessed he didn't have to know to experience it. He was breathing deeper, sitting taller, he could feel an Inner Presence again. He felt a peace stirring in his soul. He gained strength from the Presence and the peace. He was determined to continue.

He and Angelica had just had their eighth child together. He was thrilled with such a large family— especially since it was just part-time. He worked hard on the farm, but he liked that. He was outside, the older kids by his side. He was the king of his little realm. Angelica took such good care of him. Their life, as untraditional as it was, worked for them. He had pushed the guilt away a long time ago. He could rationalize anything. He didn't think this was as easy for Angelica as it was for him. He knew she still had guilt pangs. She would try to talk to him about it, but he only pretended to listen. They had all those children, surely that must mean something to her. He never talked about their future or leaving the priesthood.

He was packing to leave when he realized he was looking forward to being free. Leaving had become routine. He didn't really think whether he was looking forward to it or dreading it. He just did it. This time was different, though. He was eager to leave. There was a small town on the coast he particularly enjoyed. His parishioners loved him and took good care of him. He would be there in a few days. He was looking forward to his freedom.

The coast was beautiful, the parishioners welcoming. There was a new family in town, the Tantios. He was a doctor and they had two sons and a daughter. A party was arranged by the townspeople to meet the new family. Father Emilio was invited. There was music, singing, dancing, food and lots of wine. Emilio was having a great time reconnecting with old friends.

He was standing alone, looking at the ocean in the moonlight when someone approached him and said, "You must be Father Emilio!" He turned to see who it was when he found himself facing a woman with a come hither look in her eyes. She looked straight into his eyes. She held the gaze a little longer than usual while she touched his arm. Emilio caught his breath. She was using his tricks. Her name was Lita. They spoke for a couple of moments when they were interrupted by some friends. Emilio didn't see her again. He was called away the next day to another town.

Eventually, Emilio returned to Angelica. He was relieved to see her. Lita had shaken him. He didn't want or need that temptation. He had his pretend wife, eight children and his life as a priest. He certainly didn't need a mistress. He was very attentive to Angelica—mostly out of guilt.

Their ninth child was born nine months later.

His next visit to the small coastal town was planned. He would leave in two weeks. He both dreaded and looked forward to possibly seeing mysterious Lita again.

There is nothing drearier than a rainy day, miles away from your home with no one to talk to. Emilio was restless and worse than that, he was thinking about his life. This was his favorite town, his second home. If he ever left Angelica, this is where he would live. His mind turned to a recent conversation with her. She asked him if he would consider emigrating to America. Their relationship wouldn't have to be a secret in America. They could be free of their double life. A fresh start. She wanted the entire family including Emilio to join Rosa. Emilio wasn't shocked by her question. He knew their arrangement was hard on her. She was left for months at a time to take care of nine children and the farm. But he, on the other hand, had made a comfortable, self-serving life for himself. He had a woman who adored him, children he adored. When he needed time off from the responsibilities of a pretend wife, playing daddy and the farm, he left to attend to his parishioners. He had the best of both his worlds—and he knew it. He had no intention of changing anything or going to America.

He continued to let his mind ponder his future. What would he do if Angelica left and took their children with her? He'd need someone to cook and clean for him. He would still want to have a woman in his bed. Maybe just a mistress in every town? Too many—too much work to keep all of them happy. Since he did enjoy his time off from the responsibilities of a relationship, maybe just two or three women to take care of him in different towns. Then there was the farm. He'd sell it. He could find another place to live. He'd find a woman who had a place for him to stay. He was comfortable with his backup plan in the event Angelica ever left him. He doubted she would do that. She adored him.

His thoughts returned to that dreary day. Usually he enjoyed being in this cozy village but not today. He was restless and lonely. He didn't miss Angelica or the children. He was thinking about Lita. He was intrigued, but where was she? Who was she? Was she a good candidate for his backup plan? The day was long, and the night was endless. Thoughts about Lita, mixed in with feelings of betrayal, filled his empty bed. He needed to leave.

He was packed and ready to go when a neighbor knocked on his door. There was good news! The neighbor's beloved daughter was getting married. They wanted to have the wedding as soon as possible. Would Saturday work for Father Emilio? Emilio stayed.

He filled the next few days meeting with people, reading, swimming—anything to keep his mind occupied and his body busy. He planned to leave Sunday after Mass.

Saturday and the wedding finally arrived. So many people were there. The ceremony was beautiful, the food delicious. But no Lita. Emilio was going to leave when she suddenly appeared. "Father Emilio! You aren't leaving, are you?" Her voice was lyrically seductive. He was sure she practiced making her voice sound like that. Had he met his flirting match? Did she know men as well as he knew women? He was lured into her game. He knew what she wanted.

Emilio stayed. At sunrise he awakened in her arms in a secluded part of the beach. The night together had

185

been lustful and torrid, their attraction mutual and fiery. Lita was not apologetic. Lita always got what Lita wanted. She had wanted Emilio. She got him. But for how long?

Facing your past behavior, leaving out none of the details, reliving the good, the bad and the ugly was hard work. Emilio wanted to stop. He felt raw and vulnerable. He was so ashamed of that night with Lita. He betrayed his sweet Angelica and their children. He had betrayed himself. The only way he could see and talk to Angelica in the After Life was to go through this process. Stopping was not an option. Freedom was waiting for him at the end of this process. He made himself continue, regardless of the pain he was feeling.

Chapter Twenty-five

Angelica was enjoying another day in the After Life filled with visiting loved ones. Her life was full. She had made amends with her children and her parents. She thanked her grandparents for their support. Angelica was at long last at peace. She had forgiven herself. Pain, tension, anxiety were gone. Her time was filled with helping others.

There was a clarity in her eyes. You could tell by looking at her she was filled with healing energy. She could see the hurt in other people and help them heal. She was honored to be of assistance. There was warmth and empathy in her voice when she spoke. This was especially true if you were trying to find your way to forgiveness.

She had reconciled very old and deeply held grievances with her eldest child, Rosa. She held their open and honest relationship in her heart. Rosa was a treasure. Angelica was always happy to see her. Rosa was no longer fretting about what Emma had discovered in the Land of the Living. The lies and deceptions had been exposed in the After Life. They were coming to light in the Land of the Living. Rosa was continuing to help Emma and Elaine as much as she was allowed.

Rosa was excited today when she saw her mother. "Mom, great news! I've heard from Dad."

Angelica quit breathing. Emilio! Her precious Emilio. He had contacted their daughter? There was only one condition under which he could do that. He had forgiven himself. In the After Life, you contact someone to ask permission to see them. You schedule an "amends" meeting. That is the considerate thing to do. She was filled with joy.

"What did he say?" Angelica was trying to compose herself.

"He wants to talk to you. Will you talk to him?"

"Of course, I will. I have missed him so much. I've longed for the day I would see him again. I don't know why he has taken so long."

"I'll let him know. I'd like to see him, too. I've missed him."

Angelica waited patiently for a response from Emilio. She had waited this long, she could wait a little longer. She didn't have anything special to talk to him about. Just talking with him would be special. She had always enjoyed his company. She was sorry he was so distant when they parted. She knew she had made the best decision. He deserved to live his life in peace and in service to God.

Arrangements were made with Emilio. He was finally on his way. Eager anticipation filled Angelica's entire being. Her Emilio would be here soon. She sensed his closeness.

"You must be Angelica!" That beloved familiar voice filled the air. He used the exact same words from that magical day when they first met. Their embrace was immediate. Tender and loving. Emilio welcomed her warmth and love. He needed her courage to admit the truth. They looked into each other's eyes. Angelica knew he had something to tell her. But what?

Emilio spoke first. "I love you. I have missed you so much." Oh, how he wanted to stop there and enjoy this precious moment. She was so happy to see him. He didn't want to hurt her. Emilio contemplated not telling her the truth. Couldn't he just leave things as they were? Did she have to know? He already knew the answer. He had to tell her for his soul's healing and spiritual growth as well as hers.

"I have some things I need to tell you." Emilio explained he had deliberately poured on the charm when they first met. This was part of a plan to convince her to marry Giovanni. The plan backfired and Emilio was attracted to her. The letter with the line Angelica so loved, "I'd be a fool not to be in love with you," was written when Emilio was drunk.

He confessed that on several occasions he thought of leaving her. But he really liked the set up and the convenience of their relationship. He enjoyed being loved by her and the children. He enjoyed his time off. He admitted their relationship was based on his selfish needs.

Angelica heard the contrition in his voice. She saw the sorrow in his eyes. She listened quietly. The truth was painful, but not devastating. Angelica had worked hard on her healing. The result was inner peace. This inner peace made forgiveness easier. She forgave Emilio. But she knew there was more. She sensed the trouble he was having in telling her. She braced herself for the truth.

"There is more, isn't there, Emilio?"

"Yes," he said quietly, with tears in his eyes. So painful was this confession he couldn't look at her. He started with his thoughts around the time they had their eighth child. This is when he met Lita. He started out slowly. His voice was filled with sadness.

"I was worried you were leaving me to go to America. I was afraid to be alone. I wanted someone to take care of me. I wanted, I needed a woman in my life. I developed a backup plan. I'd have a couple of women lined up to cook, clean and sleep with me. I'm not proud of this. I recognize my selfishness.

"I met someone. Her name was Lita. She lived in that little coastal town I talked about so much. I officiated at a wedding during one of my visits there. Lita attended the wedding. I slept with her."

Emilio wanted to end the story there. The pain on Angelica's face was too much for him to bear. He was reliving the shame he felt for his selfish actions. These were the worst moments of his existence. He wanted to flee, but he knew he had to finish his confession.

"I left the next day."

"Did you see her again?" Angelica could barely speak. She already knew the answer. She remembered his distance and dwindling affection.

"Yes," Emilio's voice was an ashamed whisper. "I returned two days later. We spent the next two weeks together. I promised her I would return because I thought she expected a promise. I wasn't sure I would return to her. I told her I had some 'details' I had to work out before I could return. I was buying some time."

"Details? I was a detail? Our children were details?" Anger mixed with pain was turning into contempt. Angelica had never felt this way before. She didn't like it. This was contrary to her After Life healing experience.

"I still loved you, Angelica. I loved our children, but Lita was fun and carefree—no children, no farm, no responsibilities, but I decided I would return to you. I tried acting like nothing was amiss, but I knew you thought something was wrong. We pretended that everything was the same as before. We had our tenth child. Shortly after our son's birth, I was restless. I felt burdened. You needed more help with our large family. I had grown weary of not being the center of attention in my own house. Lita made me feel like a king."

"She treated you like a king? How did I treat you? How did you treat me? Ten children, 17 on and off years together. And you are done?" Thoughts of Lita and not his family must have filled his days and nights. Angelica could never forget how he had withdrawn his affection from her. Their kisses were mere pecks and their embraces were just an occasional friendly hug.

"I knew you noticed and you were hurting. I loved you, but I thought I wasn't in love with you anymore. I needed to move on. Lita was waiting for me—how long would she wait? How long could I stay?"

"Was there more to Emilio's lies and betrayal? Were there no limits to his selfishness?" Angelica thought to herself.

"What happened next surprised me then and still surprises me now in the After Life. You interpreted my distance and lack of sexual closeness as if I missed the priesthood. You thought I could no longer lead this divided life. I was shocked at this observation, but I went with it. This was my way out and it was your idea. You told me you were going to join our daughter Rosa in America. You were taking three of our children with you. I was saddened at the thought of not seeing my children again. I was disturbed by this, but the thought of Lita outweighed the loss of the children. I agreed to your plan. I told you I was going to the parish in the small coastal town I loved because I knew you would believe it. It was a partial truth. I lived in only partial truths."

Whatever Emilio wanted, Emilio got.

"After the last three children left, I packed my belongings, left the farm and never looked back. I went straight to Lita's open arms. We had already decided to move to a different town on the coast. Lita had found a home for us. She had everything ready and waiting for me. I never celebrated Mass again. I was never called Father Emilio again.

"The After Life has been hollow and empty. I needed this time to look inside myself. I wasn't happy with our situation. We needed to make some changes. We could have made the relationship work. I should have left the priesthood for you, but I was selfish and thought only of myself."

He wept tears of sorrow. He allowed the feelings of humiliation for his actions to surface. He was ashamed of his actions. He was in agony over the pain and confusion he had caused Angelica. She had written such a loving letter from America. He wept and wept.

Angelica now knew the whole story. The very ugly truth of Emilio's lies of omission and commission, deception and betrayal.

Angelica looked at Emilio, into those brown eyes she had so loved, and quietly, firmly ordered, "Get out."

Emilio shoulder's slumped, he hung his head and left. He wanted to beg for forgiveness. He needed her to forgive him. He was filled with remorse. He hated what he had done. He wanted to tell her the rest of the story.

His life with Lita was different than he expected. Their relationship was based on lust, not love. He missed the peace he had experienced with Angelica. He missed her insights, her companionship and laughter. He knew Angelica was better off without him. She deserved a man who would love only her. An honorable man who would keep his promises.

Emilio knew he had not been honorable. He was unfaithful to the vows he took and unfaithful to Angelica. He did not remain faithful to Lita for very long. He had many one-night stands, many flirtations.

He kept the one letter he had received from Angelica close to his heart. He had read and reread the letter so many times it was in pieces, just like his heart. The letter, so full of love and understanding, both comforted him and tortured him. Letting her go was the biggest mistake of his life. The letter was all he had left.

He remained restless and lonely until his death. He died eight years after Angelica left him. They found Angelica's letter in his hand. He was buried with it.

Chapter Twenty-six

Rosa was concerned about her mother. Angelica refused to talk to her about her meeting with Emilio. She was unusually quiet and withdrawn. Rosa sensed her mother's heart had been broken, an illusion shattered. Angelica told Rosa she needed time to think.

Angelica sat alone. She didn't want to be around anyone. She had so many thoughts and none of them were good. Her heart was broken, her soul was bruised and battered, her essence weakened. Emilio had lied and lied and lied. His selfishness knew no limits. His actions were unforgivable. He wasn't who she thought he was. He had knowingly and willingly betrayed her.

UNFORGIVABLE selfish liar. Unforgivable SELFISH liar. Unforgivable selfish LIAR. Those words echoed all around her and in her. Regardless of what she did or where she went, all she could hear was "unforgivable selfish liar." Angelica had given her power away to Emilio's story and the label she had given him, "Unforgivable Selfish Liar." Her power was her inner peace, and it was gone. She felt powerless to move forward. She had no desire to move forward. She was in agony.

There was more than pain. There was a tremendous sense of loss. She lost her Emilio. She lost her loving memories of him. She lost her "Angelica and Emilio: A Love Story That Transcended All Obstacles." He stole that from her. He made her life a lie. He made his children's lives a lie. He was an unforgivable selfish liar.

Her very identity had been stolen from her. She thought she had been his special love. The love he couldn't live without. The love that created their ten children. He ripped this away from her. She grieved the loss of her identity.

Angelica's heart and soul were paralyzed by her pain and her grief. Her inner peace had vanished. She weighed her options. She could hang on to the pain and her anger. They would fester. Angelica knew the ramifications of holding on to anger. Her inner peace would disappear. Gone would be her ability to see the happiness in her life and the good in other people. Feeding this anger was not an answer. It was not a possibility for Angelica. She knew better and she wanted to do better.

Although heartbreak and the resulting pain is possible in the After Life just like it is in the Land of the Living, both places also share a way through the pain. The way through the anger and pain was with the grace of forgiveness.

Over and over, she would ask herself, "How do I forgive the unforgivable?" Without forgiveness, she would remain paralyzed by her pain and grief. She wasn't sure she wanted to forgive him. Angelica knew that not forgiving Emilio would have an adverse effect on her. In the Land of the Living, harboring a grudge and denying forgiveness hurts everyone. Nursing a grudge can cause physical illnesses and stunt emotional and spiritual growth. In the After Life, not extending forgiveness stops your healing journey in its tracks. You'll remain stuck until you forgive.

She also knew that forgiveness does not mean you condone what a person did. They are still accountable for their actions.

There was a slight glimmer of an answer. She remembered reading something about forgiveness. "It is easy to forgive the forgivable." To forgive the unforgivable requires a special grace of spiritual and emotional maturity. The first step in acquiring this grace is the desire to forgive—even if Angelica's desire was miniscule, she needed to call upon that desire.

If Angelica wanted her peace back, she needed to nurture her miniscule desire to forgive Emilio. She started with removing the label she had placed on him. The label gave power to the story and to Emilio's actions. That power grew every time she used the label. Take away the label and the power over her would dissipate. This required discipline. She needed to change her thinking. She replaced that label with "Emilio is a child of God." That was all she could manage to do. Would that be enough to regain her power, her inner peace?

Daughter, mother, aunt, friend, wife, grandmother, those roles were also a part of her identity. She acknowledged her many good qualities. Most importantly, she remembered and embraced that she, too, was a child of God. She clung to that. It became her mantra. Angelica Caserta was and always had been much more than Emilio's lover. She was beginning to realize who she was.

Slowly, the vise-like grip of the grief and pain started to diminish. Her thinking was becoming clearer. She was healing.

Angelica still needed to forgive Emilio. First, however, she thought she needed to forgive herself. She thought she had been foolish, naïve and just plain stupid to fall for Emilio's tricks. He was an expert at lies and deception. She was angry at herself for believing him. As she started to think more clearly, she realized she had believed him because she trusted people. She had trusted him, and he betrayed her trust. She wasn't wrong or stupid.

She had loved him deeply and sincerely. That wasn't wrong or stupid either. These realizations helped restore her strong sense of self. Her power, her inner peace was returning. She was healing.

As Angelica gradually peeled back these layers of pain and grief, she could see herself as a small child. She saw herself as a child fearful she would never be loved. She hugged this child and surrounded her with love. "I love you," she whispered, "I love you."

With this revelation, she could focus on Emilio as a child of God. He was on his own individual healing journey. This journey included Emilio facing his choices and decisions. That was exactly what Angelica and everyone else in the After Life was called to do.

With the final realization that Emilio deserved to be forgiven, Angelica's inner peace was restored. This peace was deeper and stronger. Her eyes shone, her heart was full. She radiated love and peace. She was ready to see Emilio. She was ready to forgive what she thought had been the unforgivable.

∧∧∧∧∧∧∧∧∧∧∧∧∧∧∧∧∧∧∧∧∧∧∧

"Get out." "Get out." Get out." Those words were engraved upon Emilio's psyche. Etched into his soul. The one person who had loved him without reserve was in agony because of him. His self-obsession had ruined their lives. Angelica was the love of his life and he had destroyed their love. His remorse was real and genuine.

Angelica refused to see him. Every day he would ask, every day he was sent away. He wasn't going to give up. He would ask every day for all eternity if that was what it took. He wanted to hold her to tell her how sorry he was. He wanted to plead for forgiveness.

He continued to work on forgiving himself. Daily he sought inner peace. Eventually, slowly, the healing was taking place. He truly regretted his actions. He acknowledged his selfishness. He saw each selfish decision or choice he had made in his life. He made no excuses for doing what he did. Instead, he owned it and worked hard at forgiving himself and letting go of his anger and self-loathing.

He realized that behind all of those selfish acts was a very frightened little boy. A little boy afraid of never being loved. He wept and wept as he looked at this inner child. He hugged him. Emilio was on his way to an inner peace he thought he could never have.

Emilio received an invitation to visit with Angelica. Would she, could she forgive him? Would she send him away? He so wanted her to forgive him. He loved her deeply. He was in love with her. Always had been, always would be.

Angelica was standing when he walked in. She looked deeply into his eyes. She saw a small boy who was filled with fear that he would never be loved. Emilio saw a young girl who feared she would never be loved. They had each acted out this fear differently. They were finally facing these overriding fears together.

"I forgive you," whispered Angelica. She could feel her heart expanding. There was room in her heart for Emilio and his truth. Clarity returned to her thinking. She was on her healing journey again. She radiated peace and love. So did Emilio.

They held each other and wept.

They had the rest of eternity to be together. They were never going to let go of each other again.

Eventually Emilio spoke, "I just have one question"

"What is it, Emilio?"

"Who is Emma? And why does she keep talking to me?"

Chapter Twenty-seven

"Rosa! The craziest thing happened today. I heard someone talking about Antonio."

Rosa, Angelica and Emilio were visiting. This was their daily habit now. "He has agreed to help others in acclimating to the After Life. He applied to be an After Life Coach! That's like a life coach in the Land of the Living."

"What is that?"

"According to my best source of all things in the Land of the Living, my great-granddaughter, Marianne, life coaches help people set goals, make life decisions, plan their lives—that sort of thing."

"How does that translate to the After Life?"

"After Life coaches assist others in the healing journey. There has been an increase in traumatic passings. Sadly, there have been more drug overdoses and deaths resulting from gun violence. These passings are sudden. Sometimes people need help in adjusting to the After Life. A coach will help them. However, anyone who would like encouragement or guidance can sign up to have a coach."

Angelica thought it was a good idea. She and Emilio had also applied to be After Life coaches. "The first step to become a coach is an interview. Antonio had his interview."

"I wondered what he said?" Rosa was curious.

Antonio was waiting for his interview. He was nervous. He didn't know what to expect. He wanted to help others. His passing wasn't traumatic, but his life had been filled with confusion. He had learned so much in the After Life, he wanted to share his knowledge. Maybe it would help others.

The interviewer was gracious. Antonio was amazingly comfortable with her. She explained the process. "This is very straightforward, Antonio. We just want you to tell your life story. There is no right or wrong life story—no good or bad one. We want to get to know you, the real you. Please start at the beginning when you were a young boy in Italy."

"I was born in Calabria, Italy, in 1878. I have two brothers and one sister. My mother and father worked hard on their small farm. We weren't rich but we had all we needed. We attended Mass on Sundays and feast days. My mother was always very religious. I learned to read and write a little. I didn't have a formal education. I helped on the farm."

"Did you enjoy working on the farm?"

"No, I really didn't like it, but I wasn't given a choice. I did enjoy swimming and playing with my friends when I was younger. I especially enjoyed Rocco's company."

"Was he one of your brothers?"

"No, he was my best friend." Antonio paused and took a deep breath.

"How old were you?"

"I've known Rocco since I was three. We became best friends when we were eight. By the time we were twelve, we were inseparable."

"Did your parents like Rocco?"

"Yes, they wanted my sister to marry him."

"How did Rocco feel about that? How did you feel about it?"

"We weren't interested in girls. We liked hanging out together."

"What about Rocco and your sister?"

"Both families were pressuring them to marry. Rocco was only sixteen and my sister was seventeen. Rocco didn't want this. He dreaded marriage and was very depressed. He liked my sister, but he didn't want to be married to her. Our parents set the date for the wedding. Two days before the wedding Rocco disappeared. They found his body the next day. He had killed himself. He was clutching a cap I had given him.

"I was inconsolable. My parents tried to comfort me. They thought the solution was marriage. When they suggested I marry a local girl, I refused. I said I wasn't interested. My dad took me aside to talk about 'bedding' a girl, as he called it. He thought I was worried about having sexual relations and I needed to

205

give bedding a try. He told me I'd like it and then I'd want to get married. I refused.

"On my seventeenth birthday my parents gave me an ultimatum. I either marry a woman or I go to America. A few girls in our area had flirted with me. I was friendly, but I didn't want to touch or kiss them. Word was spreading that I didn't like girls. There was an implication there that horrified my parents. They were not going to be embarrassed by a son unwilling to marry. I didn't want to disappoint my parents, so I said I would leave.

"We had family and friends who had emigrated to America. I was to go to America and stay with them. I arrived in America when I was 18 years old. I visited family in various cities. I liked Youngstown, Ohio, so I stayed there. I desperately wanted to fit in. I wanted to be accepted. Eventually, I realized the only way to be accepted was to conform. This meant I had to get married. I had heard of a matchmaker, Louisa Martelli. I met with her. I said all the things I knew would be expected of me. I told her I wanted a wife and children. I really do like children, and I wanted a family. She said she knew just the girl for me.

"I was introduced to Rosa Caserta. She was beautiful but young. Louisa said she was sixteen. She looked younger. She seemed very naïve and a little lost. She could clean, cook, sew and she wanted to have children. I never told anyone, nor did I admit it to myself, but I didn't want to marry her. I didn't want to marry anyone. I wanted a home, to belong to

206

someone, to have a family. Just not now, not this way. Arrangements were made for our wedding. I thought it was odd that we weren't married in the Church. We were both Catholics, attended Mass regularly and were of age. We should be married in the Church. Louisa said the priest was very busy and didn't have time. We were married in Louisa's garden by a local official—a judge, I think.

"I had a few glasses of wine before we went to bed on our wedding night. Neither one of us knew what we were doing. We were strangers, inexperienced and frightened. I'm afraid I hurt her. I knew what I had to do to have children, so I just did it. Rosa became pregnant right away. She lost the baby. Pregnant again and lost the second baby. It was then that I found out she was only 14 when I married her. Louisa had lied. I'm not sure why she lied, but she did. Rosa was surprised that I didn't know her real age, she didn't know about the lie. Louisa should have waited until Rosa was at least sixteen. Rosa was beautiful. She could have had anyone she wanted.

"Finally, we had our first child, Antonia. I was thrilled. I had done my duty. We had a child. I had gotten a good job with the railroad. I was gone Monday through Friday. I was only home on the weekends. I liked that arrangement. I had my freedom for five days. I didn't love Rosa, but I did love my daughter. I frequently invited my friends over for parties. I craved their company. I could lose myself in playing the accordion and later the piano. I loved music. It was my creative escape. I was becoming increasingly unhappy at home. I drank and then I would drink more. I was drunk most of the weekend. I looked forward to Mondays so I could leave. I dreaded Fridays."

Antonio paused while he thought about what he just said. He would never have been so forthcoming about his life in the Land of the Living. He tried to hide his drinking. He put on a good show while he was alive. After he passed into the After Life, Antonio wanted to heal. He knew he had inflicted pain on others, and he was sorry. He was miserable in the Land of the Living. He wanted to heal his troubled soul and conflicted heart. He took a deep breath and continued his story.

"I remember the Friday I came home to Rosa dressed in a beautiful dress, her hair was perfect, the house was spotless, and she had cooked my favorite meal. I wondered why. I knew she didn't love me. I hadn't touched her for a year or more. I thought she probably wanted to have more children. I drank so I wouldn't have to think about what she was trying to do. I was right. The whole evening was invented so I would take her to bed. I had too much to drink and I lashed out at her. What I told her was true, but I was mean and unkind. I told her I hated sleeping with her. I didn't like touching her. I should have handled the situation much better. I didn't know how. I was so angry all the time, but I didn't know why—or rather I chose not to find out why. I blamed everyone around me. Mostly, I blamed Rosa.

"After my torrent of angry words, Rosa told me she was pregnant with another man's child. I was both shocked and relieved. Even through my drunken haze and blinding anger, I knew I had been saved. I said more things I regret. We came up with an arrangement that suited us. I know Rosa was confused but I didn't care. I would have a family and wouldn't have to sleep with her."

"You could accept this child as your own?" asked the interviewer.

"I wanted a family. I wanted a place where I belonged, was needed, wanted and accepted. I thought I would find that outside of myself. I thought a wife, any wife, would provide that. I thought children would provide that. I was wrong, but I didn't know that. Rosa had a daughter.

"I kept a list of Rosa's 'offenses.' Things like her hair wasn't perfectly combed, her apron was stained, her sewing was piled on a chair, I didn't like what she cooked, she didn't talk to me, she was cold and distant. I would cling to that list as a justification for my mean and cruel words. Her 'offenses' fueled my anger, or so I thought. There were moments when I was sober, I would realize how ridiculous that list was. Remorse and shame would fill my heart and mind. I couldn't stand my own behavior and thoughts, so I drank. And drank. I created a vicious, destructive cycle and I punished Rosa for it.

"A couple of years go by, and Rosa tells me she is pregnant again. I reminded her of our arrangement. She never complained. She accepted my terms. Truthfully, in my heart of hearts, I was happy for her. I wanted to tell her that but couldn't. I wish I had. I hoped she was with someone she loved. There were times when she was positively radiant. I thought she must be in love. I envied her. But instead of sharing these thoughts, I ignored her and drank more.

"Rosa went through a period of sadness. I can only guess that her lover had left her. I wanted to reach out to her, to comfort her but I didn't know how. I didn't know what to say. I hated seeing her so down. She tried to hide it, but I knew something was wrong. I only made things worse. I drank more and was miserable to be around. I continued to invite my friends to our house. I know this caused more work for Rosa, but I didn't care. I needed the distraction and an excuse to drink. I hid all my thoughts and feelings in my wine bottle. I hid myself from myself in that bottle."

The interviewer had another question. "You have described your home life. What did you do Monday through Friday when you had your 'freedom?'"

"I had some buddies who worked for the railroad. We would drink. We worked long hours. Sometimes we just had a few hours at a stop before we had to move on. I enjoyed the company of these men. I also met a couple of buddies, 'locals,' at some of our stops. We would sit around and talk. Sometimes we would go for long walks. These were the people I felt the most comfortable with. There was no pressure to act like the happy family man. There were no crude jokes about women. I never thought those jokes were funny. Some of the men engaged the services of women—if you know what I mean. I wasn't interested. I'd rather go for a walk with one of my buddies.

"A couple of years after the third child was born, Rosa seemed cheerful and lighthearted. She wanted to engage in conversations about travel, education and world events. I shut her down. There really wasn't a reason to not participate. I just wanted to stay in my misery and my wine. I guessed she might have a boyfriend who was an intellectual. She talked about learning French. I just laughed at her. I was cruel to her for no reason other than my own unhappiness. The darkness that prevailed in my head invaded my heart and soul. I was in a foul mood at home unless I surrounded myself with diversions—friends, parties and wine.

"There was a new club in town, Fuggiamo. That means 'let's escape.' Perfect, I thought. I needed to escape. I went there several times on Saturday nights with my buddies. Rosa wasn't invited. We didn't socialize outside of our house or with anyone other than her family. I became friends with a man who taught summer classes at the university. He was very handsome, smoked a pipe, charismatic. People flocked to him. He had a marvelous sense of humor. Always a joke! He spoke five languages. He would charm us with French poetry. I didn't understand what he was saying but it was sensual. I enjoyed his company. I looked forward to Saturdays because I knew I would see him. Even his name was alluring, Armani. We became close friends.

"He confided he was seeing a married woman. He said she was beautiful, witty, charming and exciting in bed. Best of all, she didn't want any strings attached to their relationship. She was in an abusive marriage with no way out. Her husband was an angry drunk. Armani provided some solace and comfort to that lonely and neglected woman. I felt sorry for her. Sadly, the summer ended, and Armani had to leave. I missed him. I wondered what happened to his sad lover.

"Then, Rosa announced very matter-of-factly that she was pregnant. As long as she followed my rules, I didn't care what she did. I had the façade of a family man with a beautiful wife, three daughters and another child on the way. The outside world must think I was a virile man. I never told Rosa that I suspected she was involved with someone. This time she had a son. I suggested the name Armani after my dear friend. She seemed taken aback. Rosa always chose the names for the children. With an odd smile on her face, she agreed to this name. She doted on the boy and encouraged him to study, to read. I enjoyed her son. He was witty and loved to tell corny jokes. He reminded me of his namesake.

"Shortly after his birth, I met a man and his wife on the train. They were so obviously in love and happy. I felt good just being around them. Their love filled those around them. This was a match made in heaven. I became friends with them.

"One day, I mentioned to the wife how much in love she seemed to be with her husband. I told her he seemed to be besotted with her, too. She thanked me and told me their relationship didn't start out that way. Theirs was an arranged marriage. They were both young, naïve and inexperienced when they married. They barely knew each other. Their story sounded like mine and Rosa's. Why was the outcome so different with them? How did they make their marriage work?

"Her husband answered, 'We wanted it to work. Divorce was not an option. We took time to get to know each other. We learned the value of seeing life from another person's perspective. We had bad days, but the good days outnumbered the bad. We were committed to staying together. Falling in love with each other was a marvelous surprise.'

"I thought and thought about what they said. I talked to a couple of friends about marriage. Some of the advice was rather crude. The bedroom played a central role in their marriages. 'Give her a couple of glasses of wine, bed her really good and she'll do whatever you want.' That was their advice.

"A few weeks went by. I had a plan. I'd invite friends to the house, we could sing and dance. I'd ask them to ask Rosa to join us. She rarely participated, but she would if someone else asked her. I'd make sure she had a couple of drinks. We'd have fun, then I'd take her to bed. My plan also included going for a walk the next day—just the two of us. We had never done that. I thought she would appreciate the gesture. I would attempt to get to know her during our walk. Walking with my close buddies always felt good. I would try that with Rosa. I tried to convince myself this is what I wanted.

"The evening went as planned. Rosa seemed like she was having a good time. I think she was a little tipsy. We ended up in my bed. I had to force myself to have sex with her. I couldn't sleep. I left the house very early that morning. I was drunk by noon. I scrapped the rest of my plan. I went home drunk and ignored Rosa the rest of the weekend. I never spoke to her about that night. I'm grateful she never mentioned it either.

"We had a beautiful daughter as a result of our one night together. We named her Aria Domenica. What a delightful child. She was the light of my life. She was creative, dramatic, loved music. She adored me and I adored her. I finally had my family—me and Aria. We would make up songs and dances. I taught her what I could on the piano. I remember she told me the accordion was old fashioned! I thought that was so funny. She filled my heart with her joy. I don't know why but she and Rosa didn't get along. They argued over everything. Aria was just a child. Rosa needed more patience with her."

"What about your other children? What about Antonia?" asked the interviewer.

"I was too hard on Antonia. I took my pain and misery out on her and Rosa. I am so sorry for my actions. I did do one good thing, though. I introduced Antonia to her husband, Nicolai."

"Antonio, what was your relationship like with Rosa's son, Armani?"

"Maybe it was because we named him Armani that he reminded me so much of him. Mani, as we called my friend, Armani, was well educated. Son Armani was very bright and enjoyed languages. He picked up Italian easily. He studied French in school. Mani met Armani. I introduced them at Fuggiamo. The two of them got along immediately.

"Armani was very close to his youngest sister, Lucia. She was Rosa's last child. Lucia was very bright. She seemed to adore her mother, although I'm not sure why. Rosa was more attached to her daughters Gianna and Minnie. Lucia used to follow Rosa around the house. She was Rosa's shadow. I think Lucia needed more attention. I know she tried to excel at everything just to win her mother's approval. Aria could be bossy with her. I told Aria she needed to be nicer to her baby sister. The two girls were close.

"Rosa didn't have any more children after Lucia. I don't know if she had any more male companionship. I didn't care. We settled into a routine of coldness and distance. I found my comfort in wine. I don't know where Rosa found comfort, or if she did.

"I started feeling ill. Eventually, I was so bad my boss made me go to the company doctor. He told me to quit drinking, but that just wasn't an option.

"I did notice the wine didn't taste the same. I thought it was the illness until I realized Rosa was diluting the wine with grape juice. I was touched by this. Rosa was trying to save me from my destructive actions. Did she care about me? I was comforted by the thought that maybe she didn't resent me. I've never told her that I caught on to what she was doing. I never thanked her for her care.

"I drank until I died. I hated leaving my Aria."

"Do you remember your passing?"

"I was surprised how attentive the children were. Antonia now had children of her own. They were so full of energy. I loved having them around me. They provided a diversion from my loneliness. They were there the day I died. Rosa was very kind to me. I didn't deserve her kindness. All the children were in the room. I could feel their love. Aria was holding my hand and singing to me. The love and her sweet voice lifted my spirits and filled my soul with peace. Then I saw Rocco and my heart was full. He came to escort me to the After Life."

"Antonio, have you talked to Rosa? Does she know your side of the story?"

"No, I haven't talked to Rosa. I have talked to Aria, though. We see each other frequently. We still sing and dance! I've made amends with Antonia. She has forgiven me for my abusive behavior. I am ready to talk to Rosa."

"If you were interviewing someone and he just told you the story you told me, what would you say to him?"

"I'd tell him his next step was to talk to Rosa, to seek her forgiveness. To explain why he did what he did."

"So you know what you need to do. Contact me after you meet with Rosa."

Antonio was reluctant to talk to Rosa. He was so sorry for his behavior. He wasn't sure she would understand. He put off writing a note asking for a meeting. He didn't know what to say to her. Communication was never easy between the two of them. That was the Land of the Living—that was then, not now. He was a different person now. Antonio was almost at peace with himself. But knowing what you should do and wanting to do it doesn't always make it easy. He needed to find the courage to talk to Rosa.

He was sitting alone, thinking, when he looked up and saw his precious Aria headed toward him. Always a pleasure to see her. He was surprised to see who was with her—Rosa. "I guess now is the time," Antonio whispered to himself.

Aria left her mother and father alone to talk. Aria and Rosa had made their peace a long time ago. They were comfortable spending time together now. Rosa loved listening to Aria sing.

Rosa looked luminous. The light around her was bright. He could sense her peace and tranquility. He hoped she would tap into that peace while he told her his story.

Antonio wasted no time. He wanted to talk before his courage disappeared. Rosa listened intently. She remained poised and serene during his version of their life together. She appreciated hearing his side of the story. Forgiveness wasn't an issue. She had forgiven him in her heart and soul a long time ago.

The tension between the two had lessened considerably after Antonio's partial confession and Rosa's forgiveness. They chatted briefly about some old friends and former neighbors. The conversation was cordial.

"I don't think I ever told you this. Rosa, your son, Armani, met his namesake."

"His namesake? I thought you just liked the name."

"I do because it reminds me of a good friend, Mani."

Mani! That was her Armani's nickname. She never used it, but others did. That is probably a common nickname, she thought to herself. It can't be the same person.

"Who was he?" she asked slowly.

"He was a character. So smart and well educated. He spoke five languages. So good looking. We used to talk for hours at Fuggiamo. We were good friends. We stayed in touch. He returned to Pittsburgh for a couple of weeks when your son Armani was about 14. I took him to meet Mani. I wanted him to meet the man I loved and admired so much. I thought they would have a lot in common. And I was right. They spoke in French, we laughed and talked. We had a great time."

"You took my 14-year-old son to a club?" Rosa was clearly annoyed.

"Yes, but only because I wanted him to meet Mani to discuss his college education. He knew more about college than we did. I told Armani not to tell you. I knew you wouldn't like it. My intentions were good, though." Antonio offered a half-smile and a pleading look.

"When you used to meet Mani at Fuggiamo, what did you talk about?" Rosa couldn't breathe. Did Antonio know? Was this his way of telling her he knew about her and Armani?

"We talked about everything! Why?"

"Was he married?"

"No. He was seeing someone. She was married but she was miserable in her marriage. Her husband drank too much and was abusive. I remember this because I felt so sorry for this woman. Armani said she was hungry for affection. He seemed to care about her. I was glad she had someone."

"Antonio…." Rosa just looked at him. Slowly, very slowly, Antonio began to realize what he had just said. Drunk husband. Abusive marriage. Lonely wife.

"Oh, no, Rosa. You were the woman I felt sorry for… it was you … my own wife." This hit him like a ton of bricks. He started to cry. He wasn't ashamed or embarrassed to cry in front of her. Remorse swept over him again and again.

Rosa put her hand on his arm. "Antonio, no more tears. I have forgiven you. Armani and I had fun together. I was happy with him. You and I had our rather unique arrangement. I was ok. I might still be annoyed that you took my son to a club, though." Her kindness touched his heart.

"Why couldn't we be honest with each other in the Land of the Living? What happened to us?" asked Rosa.

"I wasn't honest with myself. I couldn't face the truth. I was confused and frightened."

"Are you talking about getting married or our relationship? What couldn't you face?"

"Rosa, I was never attracted to women. I preferred men. I never acted on my preference. I never had a physical relationship with a man. I tried to talk myself out of it, I tried to drink it away. I never faced it until I passed over to the After Life. I always knew, I just didn't admit it to myself. I couldn't accept myself, so I buried it."

"So it wasn't me? I didn't do anything wrong? You didn't think I was repulsive?" Rosa needed to know.

"No! You are beautiful! Other men envied me— I had such a beautiful wife. I prefer men. That preference had nothing to do with you or who you are. I'm so sorry you ever thought that. I'm sorry I gave you reasons to have those thoughts. My actions toward you were unacceptable. I was angry at myself for not wanting a woman—any woman. I was angry because I thought there was something wrong with me. I was angry because I thought I didn't fit in. I was angry because I thought I was different. I was angry with God, with the world, with everything and everyone. I was angry, I drank too much. I was angry at myself because I was abusive toward you and Antonia. I am sorry." Antonio wept as he had never wept before.

Rosa looked at Antonio and saw a small boy who was afraid he wouldn't be loved. She knew how that felt. She had seen that same inner child within herself.

For the first time in their lives together, Antonio and Rosa understood each another. They hugged as friends. They had reached an important milestone in their healing and their relationship.

Chapter Twenty-eight

"I talked to Antonio," Rosa told her parents. "I am grateful for the conversation we had. I thought talking to him would be unpleasant or painful. My life with Antonio in the Land of the Living was filled with anguish, loneliness and secrets. I thought I was the only one suffering in our marriage.

"I didn't realize he was torturing himself. He didn't understand what was going on in his heart and soul. He couldn't accept himself. He didn't let anyone in— he confided in no one. He was alone in his battle with his fear and confusion. Drinking wasn't the solution. He is a different person now. We can be friends. I never thought I'd say those words!"

Emilio and Angelica looked at each other with a deep understanding of fear and the far-reaching effects of hiding from your fears. They had become experts at hiding from their fears in the Land of the Living. Now they were experiencing the joy of healing. Mutual honesty, respect and admiration fueled their relationship. They had a deep love for one another and for themselves. The journey had been a long and tough one not only for the two of them but also for Rosa and Antonio. They were happy for their daughter. They could see a new peace in her eyes.

"Antonio has accepted his sexual orientation. He seems so relaxed and comfortable with himself." Angelica was aware of her new terminology. She wondered if Rosa would comment. Rosa did not disappoint.

"Oh, Mom! You've been talking to Marianne again, haven't you? Sexual orientation? We didn't know or use that term when we were in the Land of the Living."

"Marianne is indeed a wealth of knowledge. The term is appropriate and non-shaming. Antonio is an After Life coach now. He is helping others accept themselves. They in turn can help their loved ones in the Land of the Living."

"Self-acceptance is key to a healthy life and healthy relationships. A lack of self-acceptance prevents others from accepting you as you are. Your refusal to accept who you are means you can't accept others for who *they* are. I would love to share that with everyone in the Land of the Living." Angelica and Rosa nodded in agreement with Emilio's insightful words.

Rosa added, "Antonio's confusion created a prison for him. He couldn't find a way out. He thought drinking was the key. My confusion, caused by what I thought was rejection, resulted in my trying to find comfort in the arms of other men. If we had just been honest with each other and with ourselves in the Land of the Living, our lives could have been so different."

"Our soul is on a journey. Your marriage and the healing that has taken place are just part of the journey. What ifs will not move you forward," Emilio added thoughtfully.

"If people could see what their cruel remarks, their violence and prejudice do to their very own soul, they would be appalled. The damage one inflicts on his or her own soul and psyche is swift and deep. It is one hundred times worse than what they had planned to inflict on their victim. Just one thoughtless remark damages your soul. Words are powerful." Emilio felt very strongly about this.

Angelica agreed and said, "I hope the Land of the Living will call on us to help them see peaceful alternatives to handling differences, pain and guilt."

Rosa thought about what her father had just said. She remembered Antonio's hurtful words when he lashed out at her. How they struck her to her core and undermined her sense of value and worth. Antonio had found his source of pain and anger. He had confronted it.

"Wouldn't it be acceptable to interfere when people are violent and abusive in the Land of the Living? Can't we stop it?" Rosa wanted to stop the hurling of cruel words everywhere.

"We cannot interfere with anyone's soul journey unless they ask us for help. When they do ask for help, we must be relentless in nudging them to healing and healthy actions." Emilio respected his daughter's desire to help.

"Dad, if you could share a prayer with the Land of the Living, what would it be?" Rosa was curious.

"Lord, make me an instrument of your peace. What would yours be, Angelica?"

"Dear God, let me see myself the way you see me. Rosa, what do you suggest?"

"I'd recommend starting each day with, Dear God, please guide, guard, direct and protect my every thought, word, and deed."

"Amen," they said in unison and sincerity.

Chapter Twenty-nine

Antonio's life in the After Life changed dramatically after his confession to himself and to Rosa. He was at peace with himself. He searched and found Rocco, his first and only love from his childhood. Rocco had been patiently waiting for Antonio. He knew they would eventually be together, and he was right. His faith in Antonio paid off. The two were inseparable now.

Their happiness together was contagious. Just seeing them together would renew one's belief in the power of love. They wanted to share this happiness. They wanted everyone to be as happy as they were.

They hatched a plan.

To implement it, they had to have a few more facts and details. The two conspirators worked diligently. They had to keep what they were doing a secret. They wanted to surprise someone. Someone important to Antonio.

Finally, they were ready. Today was the day.

They picked up their new friend and headed over to see Rosa. They knew she spent her afternoons with her parents. They had arranged for Rosa to be alone with them. They didn't want a large audience. They owed that to Rosa.

Rosa, Emilio and Angelica were having a conversation about some stories Marianne had shared with them. There was a lot of laughter and smiles.

"Rosa is still so beautiful," exclaimed Antonio's and Rocco's companion.

Angelica noticed the three men approaching them. "Rosa, who is that with Rocco and Antonio? Do you know him?"

Rosa turned to look in their direction. "I'm not sure...." Oh, how she wanted it to be who she thought it was.

The closer they were, the more Rosa's heart pounded, and her soul rejoiced.

"Gianni! Is that really you?"

"Yes, my beautiful Rosa, yes!"

The joy and bliss of this reunion will go down in After Life history. Their love for one another was obvious as it shone through their tears of happiness.

"Antonio! Rocco! How did you know? How did you do this? Why did you do this?" Antonio was in tears when he saw the elation on Rosa's face. His heart was full.

They just laughed. "We'll never tell. We're just glad we did."

Gianni and Rosa spent the afternoon together talking about their life in the Land of Living. He had married a very nice girl. He liked her but was not in love with her. They made the marriage work because they thought that was their duty. Their duty being complete, they were free to be with whomever they chose in the After Life. Clearly, Gianni chose Rosa.

"Gianni, I have something I have to tell you." Rosa didn't want to spoil their perfect afternoon and reunion. But she had to tell him. "You asked me if we had a child together. I told you no."

"Oh," sighed Gianni. He was disappointed.

"We didn't have one child, we had two." Rosa threw her arms around him. "Two beautiful daughters who reminded me of you each and every day."

"Two!" Gianni picked up Rosa and swung her around. "Do they look like you? Are they as beautiful as you?"

"They have your cheerfulness, your happy smile and wavy hair. They have my eyes. They are a wonderful combination of the two of us."

"Can I meet them? Do they know about me?"

"Well, I have a story to tell you."

Rosa explained everything including her arrangement with Antonio, hiding the truth for years, the family's comments that the two girls didn't look like the rest of the family. She told him everything—including her persistent granddaughter, Emma's, research.

Gianni listened intently. "Would you have told your mother any of this if Emma hadn't contacted you?"

"No, probably not."

"Then we need to thank Emma."

"I do plan on meeting her as soon as she arrives to the After Life. She keeps taunting me with "You have a lot of explaining to do, Grandmother. I will explain everything to her."

"May I meet my daughters? You've told them about me?"

"Yes and yes. I told them. Their reaction surprised me. They weren't shocked, nor did they judge me. They observed more than I realized when they were children. They noticed the lack of affection and closeness between me and Antonio. They couldn't help but notice their features were very similar to each other but so different from their siblings. Both girls married men they loved. They discovered what a loving spouse is and what a happy, successful marriage looks like. They knew I didn't have that with Antonio. They hoped I had found someone to love. And I did, I found you! I never stopped loving you. I must add one more thing. Antonio was always good to our daughters. He did his very best to be a good father."

"I will eternally be grateful to Antonio. He has brought us back together."

"Let's go find our girls."

Chapter Thirty

"Do you remember how shamelessly Mother chased after the Bellos? She was desperate for one of us to marry their son, Rico. And all that bread she baked for them. Remember? She'd bake her famous herbed bread and make me deliver it. So embarrassing! So obvious she was trying to get their attention." Gianna and her sister Minnie were visiting in the After Life.

The two sisters were close in the Land of the Living and were reunited in the After Life. They frequently spent time together sharing stories and reminiscing.

"You were the 'chosen one' Mother decided should marry Rico," laughed Minnie.

"Mother worked very hard on getting Rico's family to notice me. She even bought a new dress for me to wear to one of the afternoon socials. This was serious business to her." Gianna was laughing as she told her story.

"Why was she so enthralled with this family?"

"The Bello family had opened a new tailoring shop. Rico's father was an amazingly talented tailor. He could fit a suit like no one else. His stitching was superb, and he was an instant success. Mother wanted that lifestyle of success and money for one of her daughters. I was next in line, so I was the 'chosen one.' I didn't mind. Rico was outgoing and fun to be around."

"Were you in love with him, Gianna?"

"I loved him. Maybe not passionately in love with him, but we got along just fine. My life wasn't what Mother expected," Gianna answered her sister truthfully.

"What did she expect?"

"She thought I would live in a lovely big house with hired help. We'd have lots of children. We'd be prestigious and wealthy. Mother painted our picture based on the way she said she had lived in Italy. Our grandfather was the mayor of the community and was very influential. His family had a palazzo. That is what she thought I would have. You remember the story she used to tell us about her father, Andrea Diserta."

"I do remember the story. He was much older than our grandmother Angelica and deeply in love with her. So, did you have that kind of high society life?"

"Well, we started out our life together with that amazing wedding in 1922. My dress was stunning and cost a fortune. So did your maid of honor's dress. Do you remember them? Mother never told Father how much she spent on that wedding. The food, the cake! No one else in the family had such a wedding."

"I remember how beautiful you looked in your wedding gown. Everyone was so dressed up. Little Lucia was only seven. She couldn't get enough of that cake. Such a pretty little girl and smart, too."

"The dancing. Father and his accordion. We had such a good time. Life was good and full of promise."

"Did your life live up to those promises?"

"Not hardly. We shared the house with Rico's parents. That shouldn't have been that bad. We lived upstairs and they lived downstairs. However, his mother was domineering and demanding. She ruled both households—theirs and ours. She would sit at the bottom of the stairs and bark orders at me. She'd want me to do the laundry, fix lunch, clean the kitchen. Basically, I was her maid. My father-in-law worked all the time. Rico, on the other hand, barely worked. He preferred hanging out at Fuggiamo, a club in the neighborhood. He was good at spending his family's money, drinking and socializing. He would come home at 11 at night and expect me to fix him pasta with butter."

"Did you?"

"Yes, every night I would fix his pasta for him regardless of the time he came home."

"Was he good to your three precious daughters?"

"He loved the girls. He'd entertain them with made up stories, give them piggyback rides and play chase. He was just a big kid in an adult's body. He died a few years before I did. We see each other occasionally here in the After Life. He is the same. Lots of fun, rarely serious and still attached to his mother's apron strings."

"I guess some things just never change!"

"And what about you, dear Minnie? You married for love."

"I still don't know how Mother allowed me to marry Mateo. She was so forceful in pushing you and Rico together. I guess she was so busy with the two of you she didn't notice I was falling in love."

"He was very good to you. Everyone could see you two were in love." Gianna remembered how Mateo used to look at her sister adoringly.

"I knew the first moment I saw him that he was the one. I had been working in the canning factory for about six months. The place was dreary, cold and damp, but Mother insisted I work. One very ordinary day, I looked up and there he was. He was our new supervisor. The day went from ordinary and dreary to magical."

"A little dramatic!"

"I mean it. Our eyes connected and we both just knew. He made sure to talk to me at lunch that day and every day thereafter. We were married six months later. This was about a year after your wedding. Our wedding was much, much simpler with fewer people. I did splurge on my dress and headpiece." Minnie loved talking about her wedding gown.

"You looked gorgeous in your dress. Your headpiece was the newest thing in town. You were very fashionable." Gianna remembered her sister's wedding—especially the amazing headpiece.

"Thank you, dear Gianna. We were very happy. I quit work so we could start our family. We both wanted a dozen kids. Mateo had gotten a promotion. We were doing well financially. Then we had our darling little boy, Francesco. We called him Frank to be more American. Mateo was a recent immigrant. He wanted to fit into American society, so he changed his name to Matt. I had long ago dropped the Domenica for Minnie. We were thoroughly modern."

"I remember how happy you were when Frank was born. Such a beautiful baby."

Minnie had tears in her voice as she remembered what happened next. "I would love to have had many more children. I was only 20 years old when I started feeling so tired. I developed a terrible cough and pain in my chest. I had tuberculosis, an incurable disease. I had an infant and a loving husband I adored and now no future to look forward to. Mother graciously asked us to move in with her and Father so she could help take care of us. I didn't want to, but I couldn't take care of Matt and Frank. They couldn't take care of me. The sensible solution was to move in with them."

"Do you remember being so sick?"

"I remember the joy I felt when my son was allowed in the room. We were so cautious. We were worried I might be contagious. The memory of the illness has been erased by the love and tender care I received from everyone in the family. Armani, Aria and Lucia were still at home. They helped Mother take care of me. Father would quietly play the accordion. He wasn't feeling well, either."

"You passed over and then Father passed over months later. Tough time for all of us. I was so lonely without you. We were always so close." There was sadness in Gianna's voice.

"I know Matt had a hard time taking care of Frank. He met a woman and they married. They had a daughter. My Frankie had a half-sister." Minnie had understood Matt's need to remarry.

"I'll never forget that awful day when Matt died. It was in the newspapers. He was hit by a streetcar and was killed instantly. Frankie was only eight years old. A few months after your Matt passed over, Mother received a phone call from his new wife. She told Mother to come pick up Frankie, she couldn't take care of him any longer."

Minnie thoughtfully responded, "Poor baby boy. No mother, no father. I'm grateful Mother took him in. I know she didn't want to. Lucia, the youngest, was already eighteen. Mother was looking forward to an easier life. Free of so many children and boarders to take care of. I don't think life was very easy for Frankie. He never saw his half-sister again. He joined the military as soon as he turned eighteen. His life was good after that. He married and had four children. We see each other often now. He is a treasure!"

"He grew up thinking Antonio was his grandfather, and his musical talent came from Antonio!" Gianna was slightly amused by this.

"Little did any of them know that Antonio wasn't our biological father."

"Minnie, were you surprised when Mother told us the truth about our father?"

"No, not really. You and I used to talk about how much we looked alike but didn't look like anyone else in the family. We have so many characteristics in common. We've always been close. We seem to be able to make Mother laugh and she was easier on us than our siblings. So, no, I wasn't really surprised."

"I didn't marry for love, but Rico was good to me. We had fun together. I was saddened to hear Mother's story about Antonio. We knew he drank too much and wasn't very nice to her." Gianna was sympathetic and understanding about her mother's situation.

"Oh, Gianna! I know what you mean. After I met and married Matt, I realized that Mother and Antonio were miserable together. He was nice enough to us, but not to Mother. The distance and coldness between them were so obvious. Matt and I were completely different. We enjoyed each other's company. We spent every moment we could together. We still do!"

"I am glad Mother found love. I wish she had been free to marry our biological father, Gianni. I'm looking forward to meeting my namesake." Gianna was sincere in her desire to meet her biological father.

"Me too. I admire Mother's courage. Telling us couldn't have been easy. The truth does answer a lot of questions. I wonder if our families in the Land of the Living will ever discover the truth?"

Chapter Thirty-one

"Gianni, my son Armani is coming over today. Would you like to meet him?"

"Yes, of course, he is a part of you. He sounds fascinating."

Rosa and Gianni were now spending every minute they could together. They had shared the many joys and sorrows of their life-journeys. He knew the story of Armani's father and he looked forward to meeting son Armani.

Armani had a reason for his visit. He wanted to tell his mother he recently saw his namesake, the man Antonio introduced him to so many years ago. He was hoping she had seen Antonio so he could tell him about his friend, Mani.

Gianni sensed Rosa needed to talk to her son in private. He excused himself, leaving mother and son to talk about Mani. Rosa took a deep breath.

"I need to tell you something," Rosa started to explain when Armani interrupted.

"Mom, I already know. I just wasn't sure how to tell you I know."

"You know what?"

"I know you and Antonio were miserable together. All of us knew that—even our little Lucia mentioned it when she was a child. Antonia told us the story about

239

your leaving her at home to take care of the 'babies,' as she called them. She described your dresses. When we were adults, we suspected you had found someone, and I was the result of that liaison. I know Antonio isn't my biological father. We used to talk about this long after you passed over. Diana was part of the discussions. I'm sure she has told Elaine the stories, too."

"What convinced you that Mani is your father?" Rosa was relieved her son knew the truth.

"I met him at Fuggiamo when I was 14. Antonio took me to the club. We instantly bonded. Many years later, when I was studying at Temple University, I saw him. We had a great time together. We have similar interests, mannerisms and the same jaw line. It crossed my mind then. After Antonia told me the stories, I thought about Mani again. I dismissed it until I saw him at Pitt. I was teaching there, and he showed up at one of my classes. I looked at him and knew. I just knew. I think he might suspect it, too. He would ask about my mother. I thought that was odd since he hadn't met you."

"You are so much like your father. You do have his penchant for languages, his corny sense of humor and some of his mannerisms. You are right about my marriage to Antonio, too. We have straightened all of that out. We are friends now."

"I know he found Gianni for you. I know Antonio's story. I still consider him my dad. I have two fathers. I'm doubly blessed."

"There is more I need to tell you." Rosa proceeded to tell Armani about Lucia and Luca. Armani was easy for Rosa to talk to. They had enjoyed a special mother-son relationship in the Land of the Living. Talking to him now was even easier. She concluded the story by telling him Antonio and Aria were Antonio's daughters.

"I know you and Lucia reconciled while you were both living."

"How do you know this?"

"Lucia told me. She was going through such a rough period in her life. I finally got her to open up to me. She told me about overhearing you and Luca talking in the backyard. I promised her I wouldn't tell you I knew. Has she met Luca? Have you seen him?"

"I haven't seen him since he showed up on our doorstep when Lucia was 18 years old. I haven't looked for him. Do you think I should? What would you do?"

"I'd ask our little Lucia what she wants. Here she comes now."

"Mom! So good to see you." Lucia had been busy with other family members and hadn't seen her mother for a while. "I think Emma has been talking to you. She talks to me every day."

Rosa laughed. Lucia had blossomed in the After Life. She looked healthy and filled with joyful exuberance.

Lucia already knew about Gianni and her mother. Lucia and Rosa had a unique bond. Since Lucia knew about her biological father, Rosa had explained her other relationships after Lucia had settled into the After Life. Lucia had been so young when Antonio died, but she did remember his drinking. She knew her parents were cold and indifferent to one another. She was only a child, but she knew Antonio and her mother didn't even like one another.

"What does Emma ask you?" Rosa thought it was probably something to do with Emma's grandfather.

"She asks me about my biological father. She'd like to know who he is. I guess you've had something to do with her recent discovery? She knows his name. She is corresponding with his great-granddaughter."

"How do you know all of that? You aren't allowed to snoop."

"Emma explains everything to me. We are closer now than we ever were while I was living. Of course, the closeness is different because I no longer live in her physical world, but we are in touch frequently. Healing and forgiveness are wonderful."

"Speaking of forgiveness, do you want to meet your father?"

"I've never told you this, Mom, but I have met him."

"Here? In the After Life?"

"No," Lucia responded slowly, "I met him in the Land of the Living. I didn't want to upset you, so I never told anyone other than my husband. You remember I was transferred to Wheeling, West Virginia, after I joined the Women Ordinance Workers? There was a small diner close by the building where I worked. I'd eat there with friends several times a week. None of us had families in the area, so we'd go there as a treat. We had great fun. We became friendly with the staff and other patrons.

"Luca was one of those patrons. He heard someone call me by name. Two weeks or so after he heard my name, he approached me. He asked where I was from. That wasn't unusual. I wore an Army uniform, and the locals were very supportive of our cause."

"Did you recognize him as the man you saw me talking to in the backyard?" Rosa and Lucia could talk openly and honestly about that day now.

"I thought he looked familiar, but I didn't really think about it. I had seen him many times in the diner. I told him I was from Pittsburgh. He turned white. I'll never forget that. I was wondering what was so wrong about Pittsburgh?"

"He knew who you were." Angelica joined in the conversation. "Finally, he was face to face with his daughter."

"We talked for a few minutes. The next day, he was waiting for me when I left work. He asked if he could talk to me privately. I said he could talk to me right there. I wasn't sure what he wanted. He asked if Rosa Amorati was my mother. I knew then who he was. We ate dinner together every week for six months. He was returning to Italy to his wife and children there. He had pictures of his children, my half-siblings. He gave me one of the pictures."

"Did you see him again?"

"Only here in the After Life. He is a very nice person. I'm glad I got to know him. I don't think of him as my father. He's a friend."

"What about Antonio? What do you remember?"

"I was young when Antonio died. I have a few pleasant memories of him. And I had Sal. Sal was always good to me—to all of us. Quiet but very nice. I've seen him here in the After Life and that was very pleasant. He was a good stepfather."

"Have you met your half-siblings?"

"We have met. We get together occasionally. I have an interesting story about my half-sister, Alicia. I had a picture of her that Luca gave me. As my older daughter, Marianne, grew up she looked more and more like Alicia. The resemblance is amazing! And they have the same storytelling ability."

"Oh, that Marianne!" Rosa was laughing, remembering her granddaughter's humorous stories. "She always knows the trendiest slang words."

"Fo shizzle!" added Angelica with a big smile.

"No, Mom, oh please! No! Stop!"

"Never, Rosa, it's how Marianne and I roll. It's our jam!"

Chapter Thirty-two

"You look lost in thought, my love," Emilio observed.

"I'm thinking about patterns."

"Clothing patterns? Crochet patterns?"

"No, not that kind. I'm thinking about behavior patterns and how we hand them down to our children."

"Like what?"

"I lived a lie and had to keep secrets. I was distant and evasive with my children because I feared they would discover the truth. I wasn't honest with you about wanting you to marry me. I was afraid to say what I need and wanted. I didn't have a strong sense of self. I was afraid I'd never be loved. I inadvertently passed this down to Rosa. I didn't realize I was passing my pain to the next generation."

Emilio recognized the part his struggle with his fears and deceptions played in this replicating pattern.

Angelica continued, "Rosa did what she was told. She married a man she didn't love and she endured. She endured abuse, coldness and emotional distance from her husband. She made up a story to make herself feel better about us. She found temporary solace with other men. She had so many secrets to hide and lies to remember. She passed this down to Lucia. Lucia kept her mother's secret about Luca. This in turn prevented Lucia from telling Emma the truth.

"Emma felt this distance. Lucia treated her questions as unimportant and an intrusion in Lucia's life. Emma felt excluded. She thought her questions weren't important, therefore she wasn't important."

Emilio sighed, "Lies cause pain. We lie to cover our actions and our fears. We make terrible, hurtful decisions because we are afraid. We fear we will never be loved or accepted for who we are."

"Our soul is on a journey. How we handle the ups and downs of this journey is what is important. We have choices and decisions to make at every twist and turn. Facing our fears is the greatest gift we can give ourselves. Telling ourselves the truth unleashes a powerful energy. We need to be conscious and aware of each other and how our actions impact others. That is the message I would like to pass on to everyone in the Land of the Living and here in the After Life."

"You were a remarkable person in the Land of the Living, and you are even more amazing here!" Emilio was grateful for every moment he could spend with his Angelica.

"Did you know Antonio has been accepted as an After Life coach? I wonder what his first assignment will be?" Angelica was happy for Antonio. He had found his peace.

Chapter Thirty-three

Antonio received his first assignment as an After Life Coach. He was to prepare a talk about healing. He knew the point he wanted to make. He wasn't sure how he was going to say it.

For years he walked around feeling "less than" and disliking or loathing parts of himself. He was critical of others. He was harsh and cruel toward Rosa. He wanted to present a method for healing the damage he caused to himself and others.

He picked up a paper towel. This represented how we are born. Whole and complete. He then thought of something someone had said to him when he was young. They said he was too short. He didn't like that about himself. Antonio removed a part of the paper towel. It left a hole. As he remembered other things he didn't like about himself, he tore another hole in the paper towel.

Then he moved on to remembering hurtful words he hurled at other people—especially Rosa. He tore larger holes for those words. Being cruel to another human, telling unkind jokes, perpetuating an unflattering stereotype cause more damage to the person saying it than to the person he had intended to insult.

Soon he had a paper towel riddled with large and small holes. He had thrown away a huge part of himself. He had disowned aspects of his life. He damaged his very essence. He was only a fraction of the person he could have been. He had holes in his soul. Those holes were painful. He felt empty, aware something was missing but not knowing what, uncomfortable in his own skin and in pain—that summed up his life in the Land of the Living.

He attempted to plug these holes with cruelty toward Rosa. That didn't work—it only made him feel worse. He tried burying himself in work. The pain returned on the weekends. Then he discovered he could numb his thoughts with alcohol. This might be the answer—a few drinks might help. Maybe it did short term, he thought. But the pain always returned. When he tried more alcohol, the pain returned with greater force. He hated who he was when he was drunk, a cruel and vindictive person.

The pain he experienced was the holes calling out for attention. The disowned parts wanted to be reunited with Antonio. They wanted to return home. The louder they called, the more he drank, the angrier he became, the more he hurt others, the more he drank. He created a vicious and destructive cycle. His soul was in anguish. His self-contempt gnawed at his every thought, word, and deed.

Antonio held on to this pain for a while in the After Life, too. He wanted to feel better. He looked for a way to do this. And he found it. As he was healing, he promised himself he would help others. He would share how he healed.

His first step was to acknowledge he was in pain and needed help. His help came in the form of a simple prayer. Before saying the prayer, Antonio would remember an aspect of himself he had thrown away. He remembered his father told him he wasn't as smart as his older brother. Antonio remembered how degrading it was. He thought it must be true if his father said it. That created one of the first holes, the "I'm not smart enough" hole.

Antonio used his simple prayer, "Dear God, please shine your Healing Light on this thought, 'I'm not smart enough.'" He didn't know what healing might look like or feel like. He only knew he wanted to bring back into unity and harmony that which he had thrown away. That is what the miracle of healing is. This is what Antonio wanted and needed for himself. He wanted to share his simple but powerful prayer for bringing back into unity and harmony those pieces of himself he had thrown out. This was working for him. He knew this process would work for others.

He had taken his first step. He realized in time and with more experience that some aspects he had thrown out had multiple facets. He used the same prayer on those facets, too. "Dear God, please shine your Healing Light on my need to be cruel." "Please shine your Healing Light on my thoughts about Rosa."

His praying was persistent and consistent. He didn't let up, he didn't give up. He examined his life, his thoughts, his feelings about everything and everyone.

He liked the idea of reclaiming these parts of himself. He had felt empty for so long. The power of his self-hatred was diminishing with each prayer. He was facing his pain instead of hiding from it or numbing it. Sometimes the process was slow, other times he immediately felt better. He was taking positive action. There were positive results. He was calm. He was kinder to himself and the people around him. He started to see the good in himself and others. He wanted to share this with everyone.

This was his message. We can experience healing. We can bring back into unity and harmony those aspects of ourselves we have thrown away. We can accomplish this without knowing the how, what, when or where about healing. We just need desire and faith—and this simple prayer, "Dear God, Please shine your Healing Light on _____ (whatever we need to heal). Amen."

He was ready for his presentation. He was moving forward.

Chapter Thirty-four

"Oh good, something to look forward to! You are coming to Pittsburgh. We will go to dinner with Elaine." Diana was pleased she was going to see me and Elaine. "Bring your research about Grandmother Rosa and our Great-grandmother Angelica! I'd like to see the passenger lists and the censuses."

I was delighted Diana was interested in my research. I wasn't sure she would be delighted to discover all the fabrications and misinformation. I hoped we could put our heads together and make sense of "The Story."

Telephone calls were made, emails sent. We had a plan. The four of us would meet the first day of my visit to go over the paperwork. The second day we'd invite our first cousins once removed. We thought we might tell them what we had uncovered. We wanted more of them to take a DNA test so we would have more information.

There were big hugs and happy smiles. Finally, the four cousins were together. I talk to Diana and Elaine on a somewhat regular basis. Andrew is a dear—we just don't talk on the phone. I was so happy we were together. I was armed with all my research, documents and other paperwork. I was ready to delve into our family history. Then a thought occurred to me.

"I have an idea. Let's ask Angelica, Rosa, our parents and Marianne to join us." I knew my cousins would understand what I meant.

"How do we do that?" asked Andrew.

"Simple. Great-grandmother Angelica, Great-grandfather, Grandmother Rosa, Antonio, Aunt Antonia, Uncle Armani, Aunt Minnie, Aunt Aria, Aunt Gianna, Mom, Marianne and our grandfathers— please join us! We welcome you. We just want to know the truth. We aren't going to judge you."

"You pulled out all the stops. You invited everyone!" laughed Andrew.

"Why not? There's a lot we don't know." I brought all the old pictures that Mom had kept for years. "Do you want to look at Mom's photos? The first one was the family photo of Grandmother Rosa, Antonio and our aunts and uncles. It was taken in 1915. My mom is an infant."

"I think it is the only one of the entire family. Antonio looks so proud of his large family. He is standing with his shoulders back, chest out. He appears happy. There is Grandmother Rosa, so very prim and proper!" added Elaine.

We all laughed at that comment.

Diana mentioned Aunt Minnie and Aunt Gianna. "Everyone loved Aunt Gianna! She was so sweet and kind. She and Aunt Minnie look so much alike. It is hard to tell them apart. They don't look like their siblings."

"How old is Aunt Antonia in this picture? She doesn't look very old. Was this before she married Uncle Nicolai?" Andrew wanted to know.

Diana was Aunt Antonia's daughter. "This photo was taken right before Mom was married. Do you know the story of how they met?"

We all knew the story, but we love to listen to Diana tell stories. We asked her to tell it again.

"One Friday evening when Grandfather came home from work, he brought a man with him. He was from Italy, thirty-two years old and single. His name was Nicolai. Grandfather brought him home for one reason. He had decided that Nicolai and Antonia should be married. Mom was only sixteen. She had never been on a date. She'd never been alone with a boy. Grandfather made the decisions in the family. So Nicolai and Mom were married. He was sixteen years older than Mom. The first time they were ever alone was their wedding night. Mom and Dad were happy. They never argued. They had four children. Maybe Grandfather knew what he was doing."

"Uncle Nicolai and Aunt Antonia always did seem to care about one another. I remember visiting them. They sat next to each other on the glider on the front porch. I enjoyed talking to them." I had great memories of these visits.

"When I was growing up, Mom would stop everything she was doing to freshen up, add some make-up, put on earrings and change her dress. The four of us had to get cleaned up, too. Dad would be home soon. Dinner would be ready and waiting for him when he arrived. We did this every night." Diana was smiling as she told this story.

The next photo was of Aunt Minnie and Uncle Matt. "His real name was Mateo," said Elaine. "He changed it when he immigrated. Look how short they are! And look at that beautiful headpiece."

"I think Mom said Aunt Minnie was four feet nine inches! How tall was Aunt Lucia?" asked Diana.

"On Mom's very tallest day, she was five feet tall," I laughed. "At five-six, I'm a giant in the family."

"Do you have the picture of Aunt Aria?" Elaine was going through my stack of photos.

"Here it is! Look at her beautiful hair. Such haunting eyes. She was the beauty of the family." Diana was holding the photo.

"My mom is responsible for those long curls in Aunt Aria's hair. Mom was taller than Aunt Aria by a couple of inches." I remembered looking at that photo when I was a child. Aunt Aria always looked so mysterious to me.

"Should we talk about 'The Story?'" Elaine asked. She suggested we start at the beginning with Angelica. "What do we know about our great-grandmother?" We took turns telling "The Story." I would then add the facts as I had uncovered them.

Story: "Ten illegitimate children with a married man who was much older."

Fact: "Ten illegitimate children—true. Married man who was older—we don't know. No evidence this was true or false."

Story: "Parents disowned her. Grandparents left her money."

Fact: "We don't know—no way to find out."

Story: "Grandmother Rosa was 14 when she emigrated. They sent each child to the states when the child turned 14. Angelica arrived last with the youngest child."

Fact: "Rosa was 13. Three sisters followed Rosa— various ages. Angelica arrived third with three of her children—one of them was the youngest. Three children remained in Italy. They arrived one year after Angelica. The story isn't true."

Story: "Great-grandfather's name was Andrea Diserta."

Fact: "Andrea Diserta was four years younger than Angelica. He died 'unmarried.' He had never been married. He probably isn't our great-grandfather."

Story: "They are from Caserta, Italy. The town was named after our family."

Fact: "They are not from Caserta. There is a town named Caserta, but the naming of the town had nothing to do with our family."

Story: "He left his wife for Angelica. His wife and children lived in poverty."

Fact: "Who knows? Andrea Diserta was never married! Was he the father?"

"So none of it is true? Nothing surprises me now!" Andrew was the first to respond.

"What do we think the real story is?" Elaine asked us.

Diana offered a possibility, "We don't have the right last name for Andrea. That man could have been the mayor. Or he was a different Andrea Diserta from another part of Italy."

I referred to my research, "I looked for other Andrea Disertas. There was one but he died before he could have had ten children with Angelica. There was no evidence he lived in the same town. We have a last name for Andrea from a picture of Angelica's brother with a man known as Andrea Diserta. There isn't any proof he is that boy's father."

"Did they make up this story? Why?" Elaine asked the three of us. Elaine and I had asked each other the same question many times.

I had another possibility in mind, "What if Angelica ran a brothel? The children are from different men. Or the same man. Who knows? Angelica was a madam?"

"Why would she leave Italy? Wasn't she successful?" Andrew was laughing. He had inherited my Uncle Armani's sense of humor.

"She bought eleven tickets to the States, and she clothed, fed and housed eleven people. She must have been successful! I did read somewhere that the government had changed in Italy. There were new restrictions and taxes. Maybe that interfered with her business." I was beginning to think my theory had some merit.

"Did you hear that? Sounded like thunder. Are we expecting rain?"

"No, no rain in the forecast. That was Great-grandmother! She didn't like being called a madam," Elaine laughed.

"Any other ideas? I think she was involved with a married man just like Grandmother Rosa told the story. We have the wrong name." Diana had heard Rosa tell the story so many times. "She always told the same story with the exact same details."

"That is suspicious. Did she rehearse the story? She made it up and couldn't deviate from her fabrication. That is how she could keep track of the untruths." Maybe Andrew was right.

I had one more scandalous thought, "Maybe she had an affair with a priest."

"They had ten children? Long affair! How could they explain that?"

"Don't confuse me with the details," I laughed. "Truth is stranger than fiction."

"There—did you hear that? More thunder! Great-grandmother speaks again."

"Time for chocolate cake. Seventh Heaven-Death by Chocolate." Elaine made the all-important announcement—my favorite cake was ready to be served.

"Is the cake from Mozzi's Bakery?" I had to know.

"Is there any other bakery? Aunt Lucia's wedding cake came from Mozzi's." Diana had attended Mom's wedding.

The cake was happily devoured, and we continued discussing "The Story."

I started, "Elaine made the brilliant discovery that biologically we are half-first cousins. In our hearts we are the same as we have always been! That being said, half-first cousins mean we have different grandfathers. I've had a hard time dealing with Mom not knowing her father and the same with Uncle Armani not knowing his father. We aren't sure about the others. Although none of us knew Antonio, we grew up thinking the man standing so straight and proud in the family photo was our grandfather. He wasn't my grandfather, and he wasn't Elaine's or Andrew's grandfather."

"We'll never know about Aunt Aria because she didn't have children. We need to ask Aunt Minnie's and Aunt

Gianna's grandchildren to take a DNA test. That might help," added Elaine.

The mood had changed. We were lost in our thoughts of lies, deceptions and betrayal and the impact all of that had on us.

Something happened inside me when I found out I grew up with a lie. There was a profound sense of loss. I lost my place in the Caserta family history. I didn't know my place in my other family—in my mom's biological father's family. Who am I? My mom was the only child of that union. My sister has passed. She didn't have children. I am the only remaining link to my grandmother's and grandfather's liaison. I only have half-relatives. My husband and I don't have children. My passing will end the legacy of Rosa and Luca.

My mom lost her place, too. Her beloved brother and sisters were half-siblings. She would have hated that. She loved her family fiercely.

"I think Mom might have known Antonio wasn't her father. I have a theory. I think Mom found out sometime between high school and beauty school. Add that to Aunt Aria's poor health and Mom went into a downward spiral."

"Oh, honey, do you think so?" Diana seemed saddened by my idea.

"I think it's very possible."

"It's raining." Andrew was looking out the window. "That's weird. Sunny all day and no clouds. Guess it just blew in."

"What do we do now?" Elaine wanted to know. "More research? More DNA tests?"

"We have a possible grandfather for you and Andrew. I have a very probable one in Luca. We wait for more people to take a DNA test, more family trees to show up online. And we keep asking Grandmother Rosa for help. She has some explaining to do."

Chapter Thirty-five ·

Emilio had planned a surprise for Angelica. A family reunion! Everybody together. What an event.

"I'm so excited to see all our children, grandchildren and our great-grands. I think having this family reunion is a wonderful idea. I'm so glad you thought of it!" Angelica was beaming as she looked at Emilio.

"Everyone will be here. A rare occasion indeed."

"So much has happened in our family. Rosa and I have an honest relationship. We love each other and enjoy each other's company. I am free of the lies and deception. Most importantly, we have forgiven ourselves and each other. I wish we had forgiven one another during our time in the Land of the Living."

Hugs, kisses, smiles, laughter, tears of joy and lots of people talking. The reunion was happening. So many people. The noise level was so high, surely the Land of the Living could hear them.

Rosa was the first to hear something other than her After Life family talking and laughing. She could hear Emma.

"Mom, Gianni, do you hear that?" Rosa was trying to get their attention.

Angelica could hear her great-granddaughter asking for help. "Rosa, find your children! Emma is asking for help."

The family gathered. They remembered the panic Emma had caused when she first started researching her family. She was uncovering the truth. She knew "The Story" wasn't true. The panic was gone now. Fears faced, truths told, forgiveness extended and accepted, healing was taking place. They wanted to help their loved ones in the Land of the Living. They would have that opportunity right now. Emma had invited them to help.

The family was quiet as they listened in to Emma, Diana, Elaine and Andrew's conversation. The quietness erupted into uproarious laughter at the notion that Angelica had been a madam. They laughed so hard and so much they caused thunder in the Land of the Living.

They were silent again as they heard Emma thinking about her feelings about not knowing who her grandfather was. There were tears of sadness for the pain the lies had caused. This caused the rain. The tears of sadness turned to tears of joy as they witnessed the closeness between Diana, Elaine, Andrew and Emma. Tears of joy for their loved ones in the Land of the Living. Each tear turned to a raindrop. Each raindrop brought a message, "We are here to help. Call upon us. We are listening."

Marianne just couldn't help herself, she loved to give her grandmother a hard time. "Ohhh, Grandmother Rosa! When Emma gets here, you'll have some explaining to do!"

About the Author

Joanie Smith, an avid ancestry researcher, loves to tell family stories. While she would prefer the stories were truthful, she works with what she has been given. She is grateful she inherited a little of the Casertas' creativity and their ability to sew.

Smith is an entrepreneur who has owned several businesses including bookstores, an employment agency and a consignment store. Currently she is retired and happily sharing this retirement with her husband, Gabe, and their four-legged fur person, Sophie, in Huntington, WV.

Made in the USA
Monee, IL
28 October 2021